I0682532

AIR SERVICE BOYS IN THE BIG BATTLE

OR

SILENCING THE BIG GUNS

CHARLES AMORY BEACH

1st WORLD LIBRARY
Literary Society

Air Service Boys in the Big Battle

Charles Amory Beach

© 1st World Library – Literary Society, 2005
PO Box 2211
Fairfield, IA 52556
www.1stworldlibrary.org
First Edition

LCCN: 2006902685

Softcover ISBN: 1-4218-1819-1
Hardcover ISBN: 1-4218-1719-5
eBook ISBN: 1-4218-1919-8

Purchase *"Air Service Boys in the Big Battle"*
as a traditional bound book at:
www.1stWorldLibrary.org/purchase.asp?ISBN=1-4218-1819-1

1st World Library Literary Society is a nonprofit
organization dedicated to promoting literacy by:

- Creating a free internet library accessible from any
  computer worldwide.
- Hosting writing competitions and offering book
  publishing scholarships.

**Readers interested in supporting literacy
through sponsorship, donations or
membership please contact:
literacy@1stworldlibrary.org
Check us out at: www.1stworldlibrary.ORG
and start downloading free ebooks today.**

Air Service Boys in the Big Battle
contributed by Tim, Ed & Rodney
in support of
1st World Library Literary Society

CONTENTS

CHAPTER I

BAD NEWS FROM THE AIR

"Well, Tom, how's your head now?"

"How's my head? What do you mean? There's nothing the matter with my head," and the speaker, who wore the uniform of a French aviator, glanced up in surprise from the cot on which he was reclining in his tent near the airdromes that stretched around a great level field, not far from Paris.

"Oh, isn't there?" questioned Jack Parmly, with a smile. "Then I beg your pardon for asking, my cabbage! I beg your pardon, Sergeant Raymond!"

Tom Raymond, whose, chum had addressed him by the military title, looked curiously at his companion, and smiled at the appellation of the term cabbage. It was one of the many little tricks picked up by association with their French flying comrades, of speaking to a friend by some odd, endearing term. It might be cucumber or rose, cabbage or cart wheel - the words mattered not, it was the meaning back of them.

"Say, is anything the matter?" went on Tom, as his chum, attired like himself, but wearing an old blouse covered with oil and grease, continued to smile. "What gave you the notion that my head hurt?"

"I didn't say it hurt. I only asked how it was. The swelling hasn't begun to subside in mine yet, and I was wondering if it had in yours."

"Swelling? Subside? What in the world -"

Jack Parmly brought to a sudden termination the rapid torrent of words from the mouth of his churn by silently pointing to a small medal fastened to the uniform jacket of his friend. It was the coveted croix de guerre.

"Oh, that!" exclaimed Tom.

"Nothing else, my pickled beet!" answered Jack. "Doesn't it make your head swell up as if it would burst every time you look at it? Now don't say it doesn't, for that's the way it affects me, and I'm sure you're not very different. And every time I read the citation that goes with the medal - well, I'm just aching for a chance to show it to the folks back home, aren't you, Sergeant?"

Tom Raymond started a bit at the second use of the title.

"I see you aren't any more used to it than I am!" exclaimed Jack. "Well, it'll be a little time before we stop looking around to see if it isn't some one behind us they're talking to. So I thought I'd practice it a bit on you. And you can do the same for me. I should think, out of common politeness, you'd get up, salute and call me the same."

"Oh! Now I see what you're driving at," voiced Tom, as he glanced up from a momentary look at his medal to the face of his comrade-in-arms, or perhaps in flying would be more appropriate. "The wind's in that quarter, is it?"

"No wind at all to speak of," broke in Jack. "If you'd like to go for a fly, and see if we can bag a Boche or two, I'm with you."

"Against orders, Jack. I'd like to, but we were ordered here for rest and observation work; and you know, as well as I do, that obeying orders is just as important as sending a member of the Hun Flying Circus down where he can't do any more of his grandstand stunts. But I'm hoping the time will come when we can climb up back of our machine guns again, and do our bit to show that the little old U. S. A. is still on the map."

"I guess that time'll soon come, Tom, old man. I heard rumors that a lot of us were to be sent up nearer the front shortly, and if they don't include you and me, there'll be something doing in this camp!"

"That's what I say. So you thought I'd have a swelled head, did you, because they gave us the croix de guerre?"

"I confess I had a faint suspicion that way," admitted Jack. "Both of us being advanced to sergeants was a big step, too."

"It was," agreed Tom. "I almost wish they hadn't done it, for there are lots of others in the escadrille that deserve it fully as much, and some more, than we do."

"That's right. But you can't make these delightful Frenchmen see anything the way you want 'em to. Once they get a notion in their heads that you've done something for la belle Frame, they're your friends for life, kissing you on both cheeks and pinning medals on you wherever they'll stick."

"Well, they mean all right, Jack," said Tom. "And there aren't any braver or more lovable people on the face of the earth than these same French. They've done more and suffered more for their country than we dream of. And it's only natural that they should say 'much obliged,' in their own particular way, to any one they think is helping to free them from the Germans."

"I suppose you're right. But advancing us to sergeants would have been enough, without pinning the decorations on us and mentioning us in the order of the day, as well as giving us as fine a citation as ever was signed by a commanding general. However, it's all in the day's work, though when we flew over the German super cannons, and did our bit in helping demolish them so they couldn't shell Paris any more, we didn't think - or, at least, I didn't - that we'd be sitting here talking about it."

"Me either," agreed Tom. "But, to get down to brass tacks, what have you been doing to get into such a mess? You look like a chauffeur of the old days they tell of when they had to climb under the car to see if it needed oiling -"

"That's just about what I have been doing," admitted Jack. "When I heard the rumor that our escadrille might get orders to move at any hour, I decided that it was up to me to look MY machine over. It didn't make that nose dive just the way I wanted it to the last time I was up, and I'm not taking any chances. So I've been crawling in and around and under it -"

"While I've been lying here I taking it easy!" broke in Tom. "I don't call that fair of you, Jack," and he seemed genuinely hurt.

"Go easy now, my pickled onion!" laughed his chum. "I wasn't going to leave you out in the cold. I just came to tell you that you'd better stop looking like a moving picture of an airman, and put on some old duds to look over your own craft. And here you go and -"

"All right, old ham sandwich!" laughed Tom.

"I'll forgive you. I'm going to do the same as you, and tinker with my machine. If, as you say, we're likely to be on the job gain soon, I don't want too take any chances either. Where's that mechanician of mine? There was something wrong with my joy stick, he said, the last time I came down out of the clouds to take an enforced rest, and I might as well start with that, if there's any repairing to be done -"

Tom flung off his uniform jacket, with the two silver wings, denoting that he was a full-fledged airman, and sent an orderly to summon his chief mechanician, for each aviator had several helpers to run messages for him, as well as to see that his machine is in perfect trim.

Experts are needed to see to it that the machine and the aviator are in perfect trim, leaving for the airman himself the trying and difficult task, sometimes, of flying upside down, while he is making observations of the enemy with one eye, and fighting off a Boche with the other - ready to kill or be killed.

Sergeants Tom Raymond and Jack Parmly, chums and fellow airmen flying for France, started toward the aerodromes where their machines were kept when not in use. They were both attired now for hard and not very clean work, though the more laborious part would be done by mechanics at their orders. Still the lads themselves would leave nothing to chance. Indeed no airman does, for in very, truth his He and the success of an army may, at times, depend on the strength or weakness of a seemingly insignificant bit of wire or the continuity of a small gasoline pipe.

"Well, it'll seem good to get up in the air again," remarked Jack. "A little rest is all right, but too much is more than enough."

"Right O, my sliced liberty bond!" laughed Tom. "And now -"

Their talk was interrupted by a cheer that broke out in front of a recreation house, in reality a YMCA hut, or le Foyer du Soldat as it was called. It was where the airmen went when not on duty to read the papers, write letters and buy chocolate.

"What's up now?" asked Jack, as he and his chum looked toward the cheering squad of aviators and their assistants.

"Give it up. Let's go over and find out."

They broke into a run as the cheering continued, and then they saw hats being thrown into the air and men capering about with every evidence of joy.

"We must have won a big battle!" cried Jack.

"Seems so," agreed Tom. "Hi there! what is it?" he asked in French of a fellow aviator.

"What is it? You ask me what? Ah, joy of my life! It is you who ought to know first! It is you who should give thanks! Ah!"

"Yes, that's all right, old man," returned Jack in English. "We'll give thanks right as soon as we know what it is; but we aren't mind readers, you know, and there are so many things to guess at that there's no use in wasting the time. Tell us, like a good chap!" he begged in French, for he saw the puzzled look on the face of the aviator Tom had addressed.

"It is the best news ever!" was the answer. "The first of your brave countrymen have arrived to help us drive the Boche from France! The first American Expeditionary Force, to serve under your brave General Pershing, has reached the shores of France safely, in spite of the U-boats, and are even now marching to show themselves in Paris! Ah, is it any wonder that we rejoice? How is it you say in your own delightful country? Two cheers and a lion! Ah!"

"Tiger, my dear boy! Tiger!" laughed Jack. "And, while you're about it, you might as well make it three cheers and done with it. Not that it makes any great amount of difference in this case, but it's just the custom, my stuffed olive!"

And then he and Tom were fairly carried off their feet by the rush of enthusiastic Frenchmen to congratulate them on the good news, and to share it with them.

"Is it really true?" asked Tom. "Has any substantial part of Uncle Sam's boys really got here at last?"

He was told that such was the case. The news had just been

received at the headquarters of the flying squad to which Tom and Jack were attached. About ten thousand American soldiers were even then on French soil. Their coming had long been waited for, and the arrangements sailed in secret, and the news was known in American cities scarcely any sooner than it was in France, so careful had the military authorities been not to give the lurking German submarines a chance to torpedo the transports.

"Is not that glorious news, my friend?" asked the Frenchman who had given it to Tom and Jack.

"The best ever!" was the enthusiastic reply. And then Jack, turning to his chum, said in a low voice, as the Frenchman hurried back to the cheering throng: "You know what this means for us, of course?"

"Rather guess I do!" was the response. "It means we've got to apply for a transfer and fight under Pershing!"

"Exactly. Now how are we going to do it?"

"Oh, I fancy it will be all right. Merely a question of detail and procedure. They can't object to our wanting to fight among our own countrymen, now that enough of them are over here to make a showing. I suppose this is the first of the big army that's coming."

"I imagine so," agreed Jack. "Hurray! this is something like. There's going to be hard fighting. I realize that. But this is the beginning of the end, as I see it."

"That's what! Now, instead of tinkering over our machines, let's see the commandant and -"

Jack motioned to his chum to cease talking. Then he pointed up to the sky. There was a little speck against the blue, a speck that became larger as the two Americans watched.

"One of our fliers coming bark," remarked Tom in a low voice.

"I hope he brings more good news," returned Jack.

The approaching airman came rapidly nearer, and then the throngs that had gathered about the headquarters building to discuss the news of the arrival of the first American forces turned to watch the return of the flier.

"It's Du Boise," remarked Tom, naming an intrepid French fighter. He was one of the "aces," and had more than a score of Boche machines to his credit. "He must have been out 'on his own,' looking for a stray German."

"Yes, he and Leroy went out together," assented Jack. "But I don't see Harry's machine," and anxiously he scanned the heavens.

Harry Leroy was, like Tom and Jack, an American aviator who had lately joined the force in which the two friends had rendered such valiant service. Tom and Jack had known him on the other side - had, in fact, first met and become friendly with him at a flying school in Virginia. Leroy had suffered a slight accident which had put him out of the flying service for a year, but he had persisted, had finally been accepted, and was welcomed to France by his chums who had preceded him.

"I hope nothing has happened to Harry," murmured Tom; "but I don't see him, and it's queer Du Boise would come back without him."

"Maybe he had to - for gasoline or something," suggested Jack.

"I hope it isn't any worse than that," went on Tom. But his voice did not carry conviction.

The French aviator landed, and as he climbed out of his machine, helped by orderlies and others who rushed up, he was seen to stagger.

"Are you hurt?" asked Tom, hurrying up.

"A mere scratch-nothing, thank you," was the answer.

"Where's Harry Leroy?" Jack asked. "Did you have to leave him?"

"Ah, monsieur, I bring you bad news from the air," was the answer. "We were attacked by seven Boche machines. We each got one, and then - well, they got me - but what matters that? It is a mere nothing."

"What of Harry?" persisted Tom.

"Ah, it is of him I would speak. He is - he fell inside the enemy lines; and I had to come back for help. My petrol gave out, and I -"'

And then, pressing his hands over his breast, the brave airman staggered and fell, as a stream of blood issued from beneath his jacket.

CHAPTER II

A GIRI'S APPEAL

At once half a score of hands reached out to render aid to the stricken airman, whose blood was staining the ground where he had fallen.

Tom, seeing that his fellow aviator was more desperately wounded than the brave man had admitted, at once summoned stretcher-bearers, and he was carried to the hospital. Then all anxiously awaited the report of the surgeons, who quickly prepared to render aid to the fighter of the air.

"How is he?" asked Jack, as he and Tom, lingering near the hospital, saw one of the doctors emerge.

"He is doing very nicely," was the answer, given in French, for the two boys of the air spoke this language now with ease, if not always with absolute correctness.

"Then he isn't badly hurt?" asked Jack.

"No. The wound in his chest was only a flesh one, but it bled considerably. Two bullets from an aircraft machine gun struck ribs, and glanced off from them, but tore the flesh badly. The bleeding was held in check by the pressure DU Boise exerted on the wounds underneath his jacket, but at last he grew faint from loss of blood, and then the stream welled out. With rest and care he will be all right in a few days."

"How soon could we talk with him?" asked Tom.

"Talk with him?" asked the surgeon. "Is that necessary? He is doing very well, and -"

"Tom means ask him some questions," explained Jack. "You see, he started to tell us about our chum, Harry Leroy, who was out scouting with him. Harry was shot down, so Du Boise said, but he didn't get a chance to give any particulars, and we thought -"

"It will be a day or so before he will be able to talk to you," the surgeon said. "He is very weak, and must not be disturbed."

"Well, may we talk with him just as soon as possible?" eagerly asked Jack. "We want to find out where it was that Harry went down in his machine - out of control very likely - and if we get a chance -"

"We'd like to take it out on those that shot him down!" interrupted Torn. "Du Boise must have noticed the machines that fought him and Harry, and if we could get any idea of the Boches who were in them -"

"I see," and the surgeon bowed and smiled approval of their idea. "You want revenge. I hope you get it. As soon as we think he is able to talk," and he nodded in the direction of the hospital, "we will let you see him. Good luck to you, and confusion to the Huns!"

"Gee, but this is tough luck I" murmured Tom, as he and his chum turned away. "Just as we were getting ready to go back into the game, too! Had it all fixed up for Harry to fly with us in a sort of a triangle scheme to down the Boches, and they have to go and plump him off the map. Well, it is tough!"

"Yes, sort of takes the fun out of the good news we heard a while ago," agreed Jack. "I mean about Pershing's boys getting over here to France. I hope Harry's only wounded, instead of killed. But if the Huns have him a prisoner - good-night!"

"There's only one consolation," added Tom. "Their airmen are the best of the lot Of course that isn't saying much, but they behave a little more like human beings than the rest of the Boche gang; and if Harry has fallen a prisoner to them he'll get a bit of decent treatment, anyhow."

"That's so. We'll hope for that. And now let's go on with what we started when we saw Du Boise coming back - let's see what chance we have of being transferred to an All American escadrille."

The boys started across the field again toward the headquarters, and, nearing it, they saw, in a small motor car, a girl sitting beside the military driver. She was a pretty girl, and it needed only one glance to show that she was an American.

"Hello!" exclaimed Tom, with a low whistle. "Look who's here!"

"Do you know her?" asked Jack.

"No. Wish I did, though."

Jack glanced quickly and curiously at his chum.

"Oh, you needn't think you're the only chap that has a drag with the girls," went on Tom. "Just because Bessie Gleason -"

"Cut it out!" exclaimed Jack. "Look, she acts as though she wanted to speak to us."

The military chauffeur had alighted from the machine and was talking to one of the French aviation officers. Meanwhile the girl, left to herself, was looking about the big aviation field, with a look of wonder, mixed with alarm and nervousness. She caught sight of Tom and Jack, and a smile came to her face, making her, as Tom said afterward, the prettiest picture he had

Charles Amory Beach

seen in a long while.

"You're Americans, aren't you?" began the girl, turning frankly to them. "I know you are! And, oh, I'm in such trouble!"

Tom stepped ahead of Jack, who was taking off his cap and bowing.

"Let me have a show for my white alley," Tom murmured to his chum. "You've got one girl."

"You win," murmured Jack.

"Yes, we're from the United States," said Tom. "But it's queer to see a girl here - from America or anywhere else. How'd you get through the lines, and what can we do for you?"

"I am looking for my brother," was the answer. "I understood he was stationed here, and I managed to get passes to come to see him, but it wasn't easy work. I met this officer in his motor car, and he brought me along the last stage of the journey. Can you tell me where my brother is? His name is Harry Leroy."

Torn said afterward that he felt as though he had gone into a spinning nose dive with a Boche aviator on his tail, while Jack admitted that he felt somewhat as he did the time his gasoline pipe was severed by a Hun bullet when he was high in the air and several miles behind the enemy's lines,

"Your - your brother!" Tom managed to mutter.

"Yes, Harry Leroy. He's from the United States, too. Perhaps you know him, as I notice you are both aviators. He told me if I ever got to France to come to see him, and he mentioned the names of two young men - I have them here somewhere -"

She began to search in the depths of a little leather valise she carried, and, at that moment, the military chauffeur who had brought her to the aviation field turned to her, and spoke rapidly in French.

She understood the language, as did Tom and Jack, and at the first words her face went white. For the chauffeur informed her that her brother, Harry Leroy, whom she had come so far to see, was, even then, lying dead or wounded within the German lines.

"Oh!" the girl murmured, her fare becoming whiter and more white. "Oh - Harry!"

Then she would have fallen from the seat, only Tom leaped forward and caught her in his arms.

And while efforts were being made to restore the girl to consciousness, may I not take this opportunity of telling my new readers something of the previous books of this series, so that they may read this one more intelligently?

Torn Raymond and Jack Parmly, as related in the initial volume, "Air Service Boys Flying for France; or The Young Heroes of the Lafayette Escadrille," were Virginians. Soon after the great world conflict started, they burned with a desire to fight on the side of freedom, and it was as aviators that they desired to help.

Accordingly they went to an aviation school in Virginia, under the auspices of the Government, and there learned the rudiments of flying. Tom's father had invented an aeroplane stabilizer, but, as told in the story, the plans and other papers had been stolen by a German spy.

Tom and his chum resolved to get possession of the documents, and they kept up the search after they reached France and were made members of the Lafayette Escadrille. It was in France that they met Adolph Tuessing, the German spy.

The second volume, entitled "Air Service Boys Over the

Charles Amory Beach

Enemy's Lines; or The German Spy's Secret," takes the two young men through further adventures. They had become acquainted on the steamer with a girl named Bessie Gleason and her mother. Carl Potzfeldt, a German sailing under false colors, claimed to be a friend of Bessie and her mother, but Jack, who was more than casually interested in the girl, was suspicious of this man. And his suspicions proved correct, for Potzfeldt had planned a daring trick.

After some strenuous happenings, in which the Air Service Boys assisted, Bessie and her mother were rescued from the clutches of Potzfeldt, and went to Paris, Mrs. Gleason engaging in Red Cross work, and Bessie helping her as best she could.

Immediately preceding this present volume is the third, called "Air Service Boys Over the Rhine; or Fighting Above the Clouds."

By this time the United States had entered the great war on the side of humanity and democracy.

Then the world was startled by the news that a great German cannon was firing on Paris seventy miles away, and consternation reigned for a time. Tom and Jack had a hand in silencing the great gun, for it was they who discovered where it was hidden. Also in the third volume is related how Tom's father, who had disappeared, was found again.

The boys passed through many startling experiences with their usual bravery, so that, when the present story opens, they were taking a much needed and well-earned rest. Mr. Raymond, having accomplished his mission, had returned to the United States.

Then, as we have seen, came the news of the arrival of the first of Pershing's forces, and with it came the sad message that Harry Leroy, the chum of Torn and Jack, had fallen behind the German lines. And whether he was alive now, though wounded, or was another victim of the Hun machine guns, could not be told.

"Harry's sister couldn't have come at a worse time," remarked Tom, as he rejoined Jack, having carried the unconscious girl to the same hospital where Du Boise lay wounded.

"I should say not!" agreed Jack. "Do you really suppose she's Harry's sister?"

"I don't see Any reason to doubt it. She said so, didn't she?"

"Oh, yes, of course. I was just wondering. Say, it's going to be tough when she wakes up and realizes what's happened."

"You bet it is! This has been a tough day all around, and if it wasn't for the good news that our boys are in France I'd feel pretty rocky. But now we've got all the more incentive to get busy!" exclaimed Tom.

"What do you mean?"

"I mean get our machines in fighting trim. I'm going out and get a few Germans to make up for what they did to Harry."

"You're right! I'm with you! But what about what's her name - I mean Harry's sister?"

"I didn't hear her name. Some of the Red Cross nurses are looking after her. They promised to let me know when she came to. We can offer to help her, I suppose, being, as you might say, neighbors."

"Sure!" agreed Jack. "I'm with you. But let's go and - "

However they did not go at once, wherever it was that Jack was going to propose, for, at that moment, one of the Red Cross nurses attached to the aviation hospital carne to the door and beckoned to the boys.

"Miss Leroy is conscious now," was the message. "She wants to see you two," and the nurse smiled at them.

Tom and Jack found Miss Leroy, looking pale, but prettier than ever, sitting up in a chair. She leaned forward eagerly as they entered, and, holding out her hands, exclaimed:

"They tell me you are my brother's chums! Oh, can you not get me some news of him? Can you not let him know that I have come so far to see him? I am anxious! Oh, where is he?" and she looked from Tom to Jack, and then to Tom again.

CHAPTER III

ANXIOUS WAITING

Nellie Leroy - for such the boys learned was her name - broke the silence, that was growing tense, by asking:

"Is there any hope? Tell me, do you think there is a chance that my
brother may be alive?"

"Yes, there is, certainly!" exclaimed Tom quickly, before Jack had
an opportunity to give, possibly, a less hopeful answer.

"And if he is alive, is there a chance that he may be rescued - that I may go to him?" she went on.

"Hardly that," said Tom, slowly. "It's a wonder you ever got as near to the front as this. But as for getting past the German lines -"

"Then what can I do?" asked Nellie Leroy, eagerly. "Oh, tell me something that I can do. I'm used to hard work," she went on. "I've been a Red Cross nurse for some time, and I helped in one big explosion of a munitions plant in New Jersey before I came over. That's one reason they let me come - because I proved that I could do things I" and she did look very efficient, in spite of her paleness, in spite of her, seeming frailness. There was an indefinable air about her which showed that she would carry through whatever she undertook. "I never fainted before - never."

"It's like this," said Tom, and Jack seemed content, now, to let his chum play the chief role. "When one of us goes down in his machine back of the enemy's lines, those left over here never really know what has happened for a few days."

"And how do they know then?' she asked.

"The German airmen are more decent than some of the other Hun forces we're fighting," explained Torn. "Generally after they capture one of our escadrille members, dead or alive, they fly over our lines a few days later and drop a cap, or a glove, or something that belongs to the prisoner. Sometimes they attach a note, written by one of their airmen or from the prisoner, giving news of his condition."

"And you think they may do this in my brother's case?" asked Nellie.

"They are very likely to," assented Tom, and Jack, to whom the girl looked for confirmation, nodded, his agreement.

"How long shall we have to wait?" Harry's sister asked.

"There is no telling," said Tom "Sometimes it's a week before their airmen get a chance to fly over our lines. It all depends."

"On what?"

"On how the battle goes," answered Tom. "If there is much fighting, and many engagements in the air, the Boches don't get a chance to fly over and drop tokens of our men they may have shot down. We do the same for them, so it's six of one and a half dozen of the other. Often for a week we don't get a chance to let them know about prisoners we have, because the fighting is so severe."

"Will it be that way now?" the girl went on.

"Hard to say - we don't have the ordering of battles," replied Jack. "But it's been rather quiet for a few days, and it's likely to continue so. If it does one of their men may fly over to-morrow, or the next day, and drop something your brother wore - or even a note from him."

"Oh, I hope they do the last!" she murmured. "If I could have a note from him I'd be the happiest girl alive I I'd know, then, that he was all right."

"He may be," said Tom, trying to be hopeful. "You see Du Boise, who was with Harry when the fight took place, is himself wounded, so he can't tell us much about it."

"Yes, they told me that my brother's companion reached here badly hurt. He is so brave! I wish they would let me help take care of him. I understand a great deal about wounds, and I'm not at all afraid of the sight of blood. It was silly of me to faint just now, but - I - I couldn't help it. I'd been counting so much on seeing Harry, and when they told me he was gone -"

She covered her face with her hands, and endeavored to repress her emotion.

"You're not Harry's little sister, are you?" asked Jack, hoping to change the current of talk into other and happier channels.

"No; that's Mabel - Mab he calls her. She's younger than I. Did he often speak of her?"

"Oh, yes; and you too!" exclaimed Tom, so warmly that Nellie blushed, and the damask tint in her hitherto pale cheeks was most becoming.

"We've seen your picture, and Mab's too," went on Tom. "Harry keeps them just over his cot in the barracks. But I didn't recognize you when I saw you a little while ago in the machine. Though I might have, if so many things hadn't happened all at once, and made me sort of hazy," Tom explained.

"Then are you and my brother good friends?" asked Nellie.

"The best ever!" exclaimed Tom, and Jack warmly assented. "Not so many Americans are in this branch of the escadrille as are in others," Torn went on; "so Harry and Jack and I are a sort of little trio all by ourselves. He hardly ever goes up without us, but we are on a rest billet; and to-day he went up with Du Boise."

"If he had only come back!" sighed Nellie. "But there! I mustn't complain. Harry wouldn't let me if he were here. We both have to do our duty. Now I'm going to see what I can do to help, and not be silly and do any more fainting. I hope you'll pardon me," and she smiled at the two boys.

"Of course!" exclaimed Tom, with great emphasis, and again Miss Leroy blushed.

"Then, is to wait the only thing we can do?" she asked.

"That's all," assented Tom. "We may get a message from the clouds any day."

"And, oh! I shall pray that it may be favorable!" murmured the girl. "Perhaps I may question this Mr. Du Boise, and learn from him just what happened?" she interrogated.

"Yes, we want to talk to him ourselves, as soon as he's able to sit up," said Jack. "We want to get a shot at the Boche who downed Harry."

"So you are as fond of Harry as all that! I am glad!" exclaimed his sister. "Have you known him long?"

"We knew him slightly before we went to the flying school in

Virginia with him," said Tom. "But down there, when we started in at 'grass-cutting,' and worked our way up, we grew to know him better. Then Jack and I got our chance to come over. But Harry had a smash, and he had to wait a year."

"Yes, I know. It almost broke his heart," said Miss Leroy. "I was away at school at the time, which accounts for my not knowing more of you boys, since Harry always wrote me, or told me, about his chums. Then, when I came back after my graduation, I found that he had sailed for France."

"And maybe we weren't glad to see him!" exclaimed Tom. "It was like getting letters from home."

"Yes, I recall, now, his mentioning that he had met over here some students from the Virginia school," said Miss Leroy. "Well, after Harry sailed I was wild to go, but father and mother would not hear of it at first. Then, when the war grew worse, and I showed them that I could do hard work for the Red Cross, they consented. So I sailed, but I never expected to get like this."

"Oh, well, everything may come out all right," said Tom, as cheerfully as he could. But, in very truth, he was not very hopeful in his heart.

For once an aviator succumbs to the hail of bullets from the German machine guns in an aircraft, and his own creature of steel and wings goes hurtling down, there is only a scant chance that the disabled airman will land alive.

Of course some have done it, and, even with their machines out of control and on fire, they have lived through the awful experience. But the chances were and are against them.

Harry Leroy had been seen to go down, apparently with his machine out of control, after a fusillade of Boche bullets. This much Du Boise had said before his collapse. As to what the fallen aviator's real fate was, time alone could disclose.

"I can only wait!" sighed Nellie, as the boys took their leave. "The days will be anxious ones - days of waiting. I shall help here all I can. You'll let me know the moment there is any news - good or bad - won't you?" she begged; and her eyes filled with tears.

"We'll bring you the news at once - night or day!" exclaimed Tom, vigorously.

As he and Jack walked out of the hospital, the latter remarked:

"You seem to be a favorite there, all right, Tom, my boy. If we weren't such good chums I might be a bit jealous."

"If you feel that way I'll drop Bessie Gleason a note!" suggested Tom, quickly.

"Don't!" begged Jack. "I'll be good!"

CHAPTER IV

TRANSFERRED

One glance at the bulletin board, erected just outside their quarters at the aerodrome, told Tom and Jack what they were detailed for that day. It was the day following the arrival of Nellie Leroy at that particular place in France, only to find that her brother was missing - either dead, or alive and a prisoner behind the German lines.

"Sergeant Thomas Raymond will report to headquarters at eight o'clock, to do patrol work."

"Sergeant Jack Parmly will report to headquarters at eight o'clock for reconnaissance with a photographer, who will be detailed."

Thus read the bulletin board, and Tom and Jack, looking at it, nodded to one another, while Tom remarked:

"Got our work cut out for us all right."

"Yes," agreed Jack. "Only I wish I could change places with you. I don't like those big, heavy machines."

But orders are orders, nowhere more so than in the aviation squad, and soon the two lads, after a hearty if hasty breakfast, were ready for the day's work. They each realized that when the sun set they might either be dead, wounded or prisoners. It was a life full of eventualities.

A little later the two young airmen, in common with their comrades, were ready. Some were to do patrol work, like Tom - that is fly over and along the German lines in small swift, fighting planes, to attack a Hun machine, if any showed, and to give notice of any attack, either from the air or on the ground. The latter attacks the airmen would observe in progress and report to the commanders of infantry or batteries who could take steps to meet the attack, or even frustrate it.

Tom was assigned to a speedy Spad machine, one of great power and lightness into which he climbed. He was to fly alone, and on his machine was a machine gun of the Vickers type, which had to be aimed by directing, or pointing, the aeroplane itself at the enemy.

After Tom had given a hasty but careful look at his craft, and had assured himself of the accuracy of the report of his mechanician that it had oil and petrol, his starter took his place in front of the propeller.

"Well, Jack," called Tom to his chum, across the field, where Jack was making his preparations for taking up a photographer in a big two-seated machine, "I wish you luck."

"Same to you, old man. If you see anything of Harry, and he's alive, tell him we'll bring him back home as soon as we get a chance."

"Do you think there is any chance?" asked Tom eagerly. "I wouldn't want anything better than to get Harry away from those Boches - and make his sister happy."

"Well, there's a chance, but it's a slim one, I'm afraid," remarked Jack. "We'll talk about it after we get back. Maybe there'll be a message from the Huns about him before the day is over."

"I hope so," murmured Tom. "If those Huns only act as decently toward us as we do toward them, we'll have some news soon."

For it is true, in a number of instances that the German aviators do drop within the allied lines news of any British, French or American birdman who is captured or killed inside the German lines.

"All ready?" asked Tom of his helper.

"Switch off, gas on," was the answer.

Tom made sure that the electrical switch was disconnected. If it was left on, in "contact" as it is called, and the mechanician turned the propeller blades, there might have been a sudden starting of the engine that would have instantly kill the man. But with the switch off there could be no ignition in the cylinders.

Slowly the man turned the big blades until each cylinder was sucked full of the explosive mixture of gasoline and air.

"Contact!" he cried, and Tom threw over the switch.

Then, stepping once more up to the propeller, the man gave it a pull, and quickly released it, jumping back out of harm's way.

With a throbbing roar the engine awoke to life and the propeller spun around, a blur of indistinctness. The motor was working sweetly. Toni throttled down, assured himself that everything was working well, and then, with a wave of his hand toward Jack, began to taxi across the field, to head up into the wind. All aeroplanes are started this way - directly into the wind, to rise against it and not with it. On and on he went and then he began to climb into the air. With him climbed other birdmen who were to do patrol and contact work with him, the latter being the term used when the airship keeps in contact through signaling with infantry or artillery forces on the ground, directing their efforts against the enemy.

Having seen Tom on his way, Jack turned to his own machine. As his chum had been, Jack was dressed warmly in fur garments, even to his helmet, which was fur lined. He had on two pairs of gloves and his eyes were protected with heavy goggles. For it is very cold in the upper regions, and the swift speed of the machine sends the wind cutting into one's face so that it is impossible to see from the eyes unless they are protected.

Jack's machine was a two-seater, of a heavy and comparatively safe type - that is it was safe as long as it was not shot down by a Hun. Jack was to occupy the front seat and act as pilot, while Harris, the photographer he was to take up, sat behind him, with camera, map, pencil and paper ready at hand for the making of observations.

On either side of the photographer's seat were six loaded drums of ammunition for the Lewis gun, for use against the ruthless Hun machines. Jack had a fixed Vicker machine weapon for his use.

"Hope I get a chance to use 'em," said Harris with a grin, as he climbed into his seat, patted the loaded drums, and nodded to Jack that he was ready.

The same procedure was gone through as in the case of Tom. The man spun the propeller, and they were ready to set off. Accompanying them were two other reconnaissance planes, and four experienced fighting pilots, two of them "aces," that is men who, alone, had each brought down five or more Hun planes. The big planes, used for obtaining news, pictures, and maps of the enemy's territory, are always accompanied by fighting planes, which look out for the attacking Germans, while the other, and less speedy, craft carry the men who are to bring back vital information.

"Let her go!" exclaimed Harris to Jack, and the latter nodded to the mechanician, who, after the order of "contact," spun the blades again and they were really off, together with the others.

Up and up went Jack, sending his machine aloft in big circles as the others were doing. Before him on a support was clamped a map, similar to the one supported in front of Harris, and by consulting this Jack knew, from the instructions he had received before going up, just what part of the enemy's territory he was to cover. He was under the direction of the photographer and map-maker, for the two duties were combined in this instance.

Up and up they went. There was no talking, for though this is possible in an aeroplane when the engine is shut off, such was not now the case. But Jack knew his business.

His indicator soon showed them to be up about fourteen thousand feet, and below them an artillery duel was in progress. It was a wonderful, but terrible sight. Immediately under them, and rather too near for comfort, shrapnel was bursting all around. The "Archies," or anti-aircraft guns of the Germans, were trying to reach the French planes, and, in addition to the bullets, "woolly bears" and "flaming onions" were sent up toward them. These are two types of bursting shells, the first so named because when it explodes it does so with a cloud of black smoke and a flaming center. I have never been able to learn how the "onions" got their name, unless it is from the stench let loose by the exploding gases.

Though they were fired at viciously, neither Jack nor his companion was hit, and they continued on their way, keeping at a good height, as did their associates, until they were well over the front German lines.

Jack noticed that some of the other planes were dropping lower, to give their observers a chance to do their work, and, in response to a shove in his back from the powerful field glasses carried by Harris, Jack sent his machine down to about the nine-thousand-foot level. By a glance at the map he could see that they were now over the territory concerning which a report was wanted.

They were now under a heavy fire from the German anti-aircraft guns, but Jack was too old a hand to let this needlessly worry him. He sent his machine slipping from side to side, holding it on a level keel now and then, to enable Harris to get the photographs he wanted. In addition, the observer was also making a hasty, rough, but serviceable map of what he saw.

Jack glanced down, and noted a German supply train puffing its way along toward some depot, and he headed toward this to give Harris a chance to note whether there were any supplies of ammunition, or anything else, that might profitably be bombed later. He also saw several columns of German infantry on the march, but as they were not out to make an attack now, they had to watch the Huns moving up to the front line trenches, there later, doubtless, to give battle.

Back and forth over the German lines flew Jack, Harris meanwhile doing important observation work. As Jack went lower he came under a fiercer fire of the batteries, until, it became so hot, from the shrapnel bursts, that he fain would have turned and made for home. But orders were orders, and Harris had not yet indicated that he had enough.

Twisting and turning, to make as poor a mark as possible for the enemy guns, Jack sent his machine here and there. The other pilots were doing the same. Machine guns were now opening up on them, and once the burst of fire came so close that Jack began to "zoom." That is he sent his craft up and down sharply, like the curves and bumps in a roller-coaster railway track.

By this time the leading plane gave the signal for the return, and, thankful enough that they had not been hit, Jack swung about. But the danger was not over. They had yet to pass across the enemy's front line trenches, and when Harris signaled Jack to go down low in crossing the lad wondered what the order was for. It was merely that the observer wanted to see what was going on there so he could report.

They went down to within a mile of the earth, and several times the plane was struck by pieces of shrapnel or bullets from machine guns. Twice flying bits of metal came uncomfortably close to Jack, but he was kept too busy with the management of his machine to more than notice them. Harris was working hard at the camera and the maps.

Then, suddenly, came the danger signal from the leading plane, and only just in time. Out from the German hangars came several battle machines. Harris dropped his pencil and got ready the automatic gun, but it was not needed, for, after approaching as though about to attack, the Huns suddenly veered off. Later the reason for this became known. A squadron of French planes had arisen as swiftly to give battle, and however brave the Hun may be when he outnumbers the enemy, he had yet to be known to take on a combat against odds.

So Jack and his observer safely reached the aerodrome again, bringing back much valuable information.

"Is Tom here yet?" was Jack's first inquiry after he had divested himself of his togs and men had rushed to the developing room the camera with its precious plates.

"Not yet," some of his chums told him. "They're having a fight upstairs I guess."

Jack nodded and looked anxiously in the direction in which Tom was last seen.

It was an hour before the scouting airplanes came back, and one was so badly shot up and its pilot so wounded that it only just managed to get over the French lines before almost crashing to earth.

"Are you all right, Tom?" cried Jack, as he rushed up to his chum, when he saw the latter getting out of his craft, rather stiff from the cold.

"Yes. They went at me hard - two of 'em but I think I accounted for one, unless he went into a spinning nose dive just to fool me."

"Oh, they'll do that if they get the chance."

"I know," assented Tom. "Hello!" he exclaimed as he noticed a splintered strut near his head. "That came rather close."

And indeed it had. For a bullet, or a piece of shrapnel, has plowed a furrow in the bit of supporting wood, not two inches away from Tom's head, though in the excitement of the fight he had not noticed it.

There had been a fight in the upper air and one of the French machines had not come home.

"Another man to await news of," said the flight lieutenant sadly, when the report reached him. "That's two in two days."

"No news of Leroy yet?" asked Tom and Jack, as they went out of headquarters after reporting.

"None, I am sorry to say. It is barely possible that he landed in some lonely spot and is still hiding out - if he is not killed. But I understand you two young men had something to request of me. I can give you some attention now," went on the commander of their squadron.

"We want to be transferred!" exclaimed Tom. "Now, that Pershing's men are here -"

"I understand," was the answer. "You want to fight with your countrymen. Well, I would do the same. I will see if I can get you transferred, though I shall much regret losing you."

He was as good as his word, and a week later, following some strenuous fights in the air, Tom and Jack received notice that they could report to the first United States air squadron, which was then being formed on that part of the front where the first of Pershing's men were brigaded with, the French and British armies.

Du Boise, who had brought word back of the fate that had befallen Harry Leroy, sent for Tom and Jack when it became known that they were to leave.

"Shall I ever see you again?" he asked wistfully.

"To be sure," was Tom's hearty answer. "We aren't going far away, and we'll fly over to see you the first chance we get. Besides, we're going to depend on you to give us some information regarding Leroy. If the Huns drop any message at all they'll do it at this aerodrome."

"Yes, I believe you're right," assented Du Boise, trying not to show the pain that racked him. "But it's so long, now, I begin to believe he must be dead, and either the Huns don't know it or they aren't going to bother to send us word. But I'll let you know as soon as I hear anything."

"Is his sister here yet?" asked Jack, for Tom and he had been too busy the last two days, getting ready to shift their quarters, to call on Nellie Leroy.

"She has gone back to Paris," answered Du Boise. "There was no place for her here. I can give you her address. I promised to let her know in case I got word about her brother."

"I wish you would give me the address!" exclaimed Tom eagerly, and his chum smiled at his show of interest.

CHAPTER V

THE RESOLVE

"Well, to-morrow, if all goes well, we'll be with Pershing's boys," remarked Jack, as he and Tom were sitting in their quarters after breakfast, the last day but one they were to spend in the Lafayette Escadrille with which they had so long been associated.

"That's so. We'll soon be on the firing line with Uncle Sam," agreed Tom. "Of course we've been with him, in a way, ever since we've been fighting, for it's all in the same cause. But there'll be a little more satisfaction in being 'on our own,' as the English say."

"You're right. What's on for to-day?" asked Jack.

"Haven't the least idea. But here comes a messenger now."

As Tom spoke he glanced from a window and saw an orderly coming toward their quarters. The man seemed in a hurry.

"Something's up!" decided Jack. "Maybe they've got word from poor Harry."

"I'm beginning to give him up," said Tom. "If they were going to let us have any news of him they'd have done it long ago - the beasts!" and he fairly snarled out the words.

"Still I'm not giving up," returned Jack. "I can't explain why, but I have a feeling that, some day, we'll see Harry Leroy again."

Tom shook his head.

"I wish I could be as hopeful as you," he said. "Maybe we'll see him again - or his grave. But I want to say, right now, that if ever I have a chance at the Hun who shot him down, that Hun Will get no mercy from me!"

"Same here!" echoed Jack. "But here comes the orderly."

The man entered and handed Jack a slip of paper. It was from the commander of their squadron, and said, in effect, that though Tom and Jack were no longer under his orders, having been duly transferred to another sector, yet he would be obliged if they would call on him, at his quarters.

"Maybe he has news!" exclaimed Jack, eagerly.

Again Tom shook his head.

"He'd have said so if that was the case," he remarked as he and his chum prepared to report at headquarters, telling the messenger they would soon follow him.

"Ah, young gentlemen, I am glad to see, you!" exclaimed the commander, and it was as friends that he greeted Tom and Jack and not as military subordinates. "Do you want to do me one last favor?"

"A thousand if we can!" exclaimed Jack, for he and Tom had caught something of the French enthusiasm of manner, from having associated with the brave airmen so long.

"Good! Then I shall feel free to ask. Know then, that I am a little short-handed in experienced airmen. The Huns have taken heavy toll of us these last few days," he went on sorrowfully, and Torn and Jack knew this to be so, for two aces, as well as some pilots of lesser magnitude, had been shot down. But ample revenge had been taken.

"By all rights you are entitled to a holiday before you join your new command, under the great Pershing," went on the flight commander. "However, as I need the services of two brave men to do patrol duty, I appeal to you. There is a machine gun nest, somewhere in the Boche lines, that has been doing terrible execution. If you could find the battery, and signal its location, we might destroy it with our artillery, and so save many brave lives for France," he went on. "I do not like to ask you - "

"Tell 'em to get out the machines!" interrupted Jack. "We were just wishing we could do something to make up for the loss of Harry Leroy, and this may give it to us. You haven't heard anything of him, have you?" he asked.

The commander shook his head.

"I fear we shall never hear from him," he said. "Though only yesterday we received back some of the effects of one of our men who was shot down behind their lines. I can not understand in Leroy's case."

"Well, we'll make 'em pay a price all right!" declared Tom. "And now what about this machine gun nest?"

The commander gave them such information as he had. It was not unusual, such work as Tom and Jack were about to undertake. As the officer had said, they were practically exempt now that they were about to be transferred. But they had volunteered, as he probably knew they would.

Two speedy Spad machines were run out for the use of Tom and Jack, each one to have his own, for the work they were to do was dangerous and they would have need of speed.

They looked over the machine guns to see that they were in shape for quick work, and as the one on the machine Tom selected had congealed oil on the mechanism, having lately returned from a high flight, another weapon was quickly attached. Nothing receives more care and attention at an aerodrome than the motor of the plane and the mechanism of the machine gun. The latter are constructed so as to be easily and quickly mounted and dismounted, and at the close of each day's flight the guns are carefully inspected and cleaned ready for the morrow.

"Locate the machine gun battery if you can," was the parting request to Tom and Jack as they prepared to ascend. "Send back word of the location as nearly as you can to our batteries, and the men there will see to the rest."

"We will!" cried the Americans.

Locating a machine gun nest is not as easy as picking out a hostile battery of heavier guns, for the former, being smaller, are more easily concealed.

But Tom and Jack would, of course, do their best to help out their friends, the French. Over toward the German lines they flew, and began to scan with eager eyes the ground below them. They could not fly at a very great height, as they needed to be low down in order to see, and in this position they were a mark for the anti-aircraft guns of the Huns.

They had no sooner got over the enemy trenches, and were peering about for the possible location of the machine gun emplacement, when they were greeted with bursts of fire. But by skillfully dodging they escaped being hit themselves, though their machines were struck. The two chums were separated by about a mile, for they wanted to cover as much ground as possible.

At last, to his great delight, Tom saw a burst of smoke from a building that had been so demolished by shell fire that it seemed nothing could now inhabit it. But the truth was soon apparent. The machine gun nest was in the cellar, and from there, well hidden, had been doing terrible execution on the allied forces. Pausing only to make sure of his surmise, Tom began to tap out on his wireless key the location of the hidden machine gun nest.

Most of the aeroplanes carry a wireless outfit. An aerial trails after them, and the electric impulses, dripping off this, so to speak, reach the battery headquarters. Owing to the noise caused by the motor of the airship, no message can be sent to the airman in return, and he has to depend on signs made on the ground, arrows or circles in white by day and lighted signals at night, to make sure that his messages are being received and understood.

The Allies, of course, possess maps of every sector of the enemy's front, so that by reference to these maps the aircraft observer can send back word as to almost the precise location of the battery which it is desired to destroy.

Quickly tapping out word where the battery was located, Tom awaited developments, circling around the spot in his machine. He was fired at from guns on the ground below, but, to his delight, no hostile planes rose to give him combat. A glance across the expanse, however, showed that Jack was engaging two.

"He's keeping them from me!" thought Tom, and his heart was heavy, for he realized that Jack might be killed. However, it was the fortune of war. As long as the Hun planes were fighting Jack they would not molest him, and he might have time to send word to the French battery that would result in the destruction of the Hun machine nest.

There came a burst of fire from the Allied lines he had left, and Tom saw a shell land to the left and far beyond the Hun battery hidden in the old ruins. He at once sent back a correcting signal.

The more a gun is elevated up to a certain point, the farther it shoots. Forty-three degrees is about the maximum elevation. Again, if a gun is elevated too high it shoots over instead of directly at the target aimed at. It is then necessary to lower the elevation. Tom has seen that the guns of the French battery, which were seeking to destroy the machine gun nest were shooting beyond the mark. Accordingly they were told to depress their muzzles.

This was done, but still the shells fell to the left, and an additional correction was necessary. It is comparatively easy to make corrections in elevation or depression that will rectify errors in shooting short of or beyond a mark. It is not so easy to make the same corrections in what, for the sake of simplicity, may be called right or left errors, that is horizontal firing. To make these corrections it becomes needful to inscribe imaginary circles about the target, in this case the machine gun nest.

These circles are named from the letters of the alphabet. For instance, a circle drawn three hundred yards around a Hun battery as a center might be designated A. The next circle, two hundred yards less in size, would be B and so on, down to perhaps five yards, and that is getting very close.

The circles are further divided, as a piece of pie is cut, into twelve sectors, and numbered from 1 to 12. The last sector is due north, while 6 would be due south, 3 east, and 9 west, with the other figures for northeast, southwest, and so on.

If a shot falls in the fifty-yard circle, indicated by the letter D, but to the southwest of the mark, it is necessary to indicate that by sending the message "D-7," which would mean that, speaking according to the points of the compass, the missile had fallen within fifty yards of the mark, but to the south-southwest of it, and correction must be made accordingly.

Tom watched the falling shells. They came nearer and nearer to the hidden battery and at last he saw one fall plump where it was needed. There was a great puff of smoke, and when it had blown away there was only a hole in the ground where the ruins had been hiding the machine guns.

Tom's work was done, and he flew off to the aid of Jack, who had overcome one Hun, sending his plane crashing to earth. But the other, an expert fighter, was pressing him hard until Ton opened up on him with his machine gun. Then the German, having no stomach for odds, turned tail and flew toward his own lines.

"Good for you, Tom!" yelled Jack, though he knew his chum could not hear him because of the noise of the motor.

Together the two lads, who had engaged in their last battle strictly with the French, made for their aerodrome, reaching it safely, though, as it was learned when Jack dismounted, he had received a slight bullet wound in one side from a missile sent by one of the attacking planes. But the hurt was only a flesh wound; though, had it gone an inch to one side, it would have ended Jack's fighting days.

Hearty and enthusiastic were the congratulations that greeted the exploit of Torn in finding the German machine gun nest that had been such a menace, nor were the thanks to Jack any less warm, for without his help Tom could never have maintained his position, and sent back corrections to the battery which brought about the desired result.

"It is a glorious end to your stay with us," said the commander, with shining eyes, as he congratulated them.

There was a little impromptu banquet in the quarters that night, and Tom and Jack were bidden God-speed to their new quarters.

"There's only one thing I want to say!" said Jack quietly, as he rose in response to a demand that he talk.

"Let us hear it, my slice of bacon!" called a jolly ace.

"It's this," went on Jack. "That I hereby resolve that if we - I mean Tom and I - can't rescue our comrade, Harry Leroy, from the Huns - provided he's alive - that we'll take a toll of five Germans for him - or as many, up to that number, as we can shoot down before they get us. Five German fliers is the price of Harry Leroy, who was worth a hundred of them!"

"Bravo! Hurrah! So he was! Death to the Huns!" were the cries.

Torn Raymond sprang to his feet

"What Jack says I say!" he cried. "But I double the toll. If Harry Leroy is dead he leaves a sister. You all saw her here! Well, I'll get five Huns for her, and that makes ten between Jack and me!"

"Success to you!" cried several.

With this resolve to spur them on, Tom and Jack bade their bravo comrades farewell and started for Paris, whence they were to journey to the headquarters of General Pershing and his men.

CHAPTER VI

IN PARIS

Attired in their natty uniforms of the La Fayette Escadrille, which they had not discarded, with the double wings showing that they were fully qualified pilots and aviators, Jack Parmly and Tom Raymond attracted no little attention as, several hours after leaving their places on the battle front, they arrived in Paris. They were to have a few days rest before joining the newly formed American aviation section which, as yet, was hardly ready for active work.

"Well, they're here!" suddenly cried Tom, as he and Jack made their way out of the station to seek a modest hotel where they might stay until time for them to report.

"Who? Where? I don't see 'em!" exclaimed Jack, as he crowded to the side of his chum, murmurs from a group of French persons testifying to the esteem in which the American lads were held.

"There!" went on Tom, pointing. "See some of our doughboys! And maybe the crowds aren't glad to have 'em here! It's great, I tell you, great!"

As he spoke he pointed to several khaki-clad infantrymen, some of the first of the ten thousand Americans lads that were sent over to "take the germ out of Germany." The Americans were rather at a loss, but they seemed masters of themselves, and laughed and talked with glee as they gazed on the unfamiliar scenes. They, too, were enjoying a holiday before being sent on to be billeted with the French or British troops.

"Come on, let's talk to 'em!" cried Tom, enthusiastically. "It's as good as a letter from home to see 'em!"

"I thought you meant you saw - er - Bessie and her mother," returned Jack, and there was a little disappointment in his voice.

"Oh, we'll see them soon enough, if they're still in Paris," said Tom, gazing curiously at his chum. "But they don't know we are coming here."

"Yes, they do," said Jack, quietly.

"They do? Then you must have written."

"Of course. Don't you want to see them before we get shipped off to a new sector?"

"Why, yes. Just now, though, I'm anxious to hear some good, old United States talk. Come on, let's speak to 'em. There's one bunch that seems to be in trouble."

But the trouble was only because some of Pershing's boys - as they were generally called wanted to make some purchases at a candy shop and did not know enough of the language to make their meaning clear. It was a good-natured misunderstanding, and both the French shop-keeper and his helper and the doughboys were laughing over it.

"Hello, boys! Glad to see you! Can we help you out?" asked Tom, as he and Jack joined the group.

The infantrymen whirled about.

"Well, for the love of the Mason an' Dixon line! is there

somebody heah who can speak our talk?" cried one lad, his accent unmistakably marking him as Southern.

"Guess we can help you out," said Jack. "We're from God's country, too," and in an instant the were surrounded and being shaken hands with on all sides, while a perfect barrage of questions was fired at them.

Then, when the little misunderstanding at the candy shop had been straightened out, Tom and Jack told something of who they were, mentioning the fact that they were soon to fight directly under the stars and stripes, information which drew whoops of delight from the enthusiastic infantrymen.

"But say, friend," called out one of the new American soldiers, "can you sling enough of this lingo to lead us to a place where we can get ham and eggs? I mean a real eating place, not just a coffee stand. I've been opening my mouth, champing my jaws and rubbing my stomach all day, trying to tell these folks that I'm hungry and want a square meal, and half the time they think I need a doctor. Lead me to a hash foundry."

"All right, come on with us!" laughed Tom. "We're going to eat, too. I guess we can fix you up."

The two aviators had been in Paris before and they knew their way about, as well as being able to speak the language fairly well. Soon, with their new friends from overseas, they were seated in a quiet restaurant, where substantial food could be had in spite of war prices. And then it was give and take, question and answer, until a group of Parisians that had gathered about turned away shaking their heads at their inability to understand the strange talk. But they were well aware of the spirit of it all, and more than one silently blessed the Americans as among the saviors of France.

The wonderful city seemed filled with soldiers of all the Allied nations, and most conspicuous, because of recent events, were the khaki-clad boys who were soon to fight under Pershing.

Having seen that the little contingent they had taken under their protection got what they wanted, Tom and Jack, bidding them farewell, but promising to see them again soon, went to their hotel.

And, their baggage arriving, Jack proceeded to get ready for a bath and a general furbishing. He seemed very particular.

"Going out?" asked Tom.

"Why - er - yes. Thought I'd go to call on Bessie Gleason. This is her night off duty - hers and her mother's."

"How do you know?"

"Well - er - she said so. Want to come?"

"Nixy. Two's company and you know what three is."

"Oh, come on! Mrs. Gleason will be glad to see you."

"Well, I suppose I might," assented Tom, who, truth to tell, did not relish spending the evening alone.

Bessie and her mother had, of late, been assigned as Red Cross workers to a hospital in the environs of Paris, and ant times they could come into the city for a rest. They maintained a modest apartment not far from the hotel where Tom and Jack had put up, and soon the two lads found themselves at the place where their friends lived.

"Oh, I'm so glad you both came!" exclaimed Bessie as she greeted them. "We have company and -"

"Company!" exclaimed Jack, drawing back.

"Yes, the dearest, most delightful girl you ever -"

"Girl!" exclaimed Tom.

"Yes. But come on in and meet her. I'm sure you'll both fall in love with her."

Jack was on the point of saying something, but thought better of it, and a moment later, to the great surprise of himself and Torn, they were facing Nellie Leroy.

CHAPTER VII

THE AMERICAN FRONT

Tom and Jack bowed. In fact, so great was their surprise at first that this was all they could do. Then they stared first at Bessie and then at the other girl - the sister of Harry, their chum, who was somewhere, dead or alive, behind the German lines.

"Well, aren't you glad to see her?" demanded Bessie. "I thought I'd surprise you."

"You have," said Jack. "Very much!"

"Glad to see her - why - of course. But - but - how -"

Tom found himself stuttering and stammering, so he stopped, and stared so hard at Nellie Leroy that she smiled, though rather sadly, for it was plain to be seen her grief over the possible death of her brother weighed down on her. And then she went on:

"Well, I'm real - I'm not a dream, Mr. Raymond."

"So I see - I mean I'm glad to see it - I mean - oh, I don't know what I do mean!" he finished desperately. "Did you know she was going to be here? Was that the reason you asked me to come?" he inquired of Jack.

"Hadn't the least notion in the world," answered Jack. "I'm as much surprised as you are."

"Well, we'll take pity on you and tell you all about it," said Bessie. "Mother, here are the boys," she called; and Mrs. Gleason, who had suffered so much since having been saved from the Lusitania and afterward rescued by air craft from the lonely castle, came out of her room to greet the boys.

They were as glad to see her as she was to meet them again, and for a time there was an interchange of talk. Then Mrs. Gleason withdrew to leave the young people to themselves.

"Well, go on, tell us all about it!" begged Tom, who could not take his eyes off Nellie Leroy. "How did she get here?" and he indicated Harry's sister.

"He talks of me as though I were some specimen!" laughed the girl. "But go on - tell him, Bessie."

"Well, it isn't much of a story," said Bessie Gleason. "Nellie started to do Red Cross work, as mother and I are doing, and she was assigned to the hospital where we were."

"This was after I heard the terrible news about poor Harry at your escadrille," Nellie broke in, to say to Tom and Jack. "I - I suppose you haven't had any - word?" she faltered.

"Not yet," Jack answered. "But we may get it any day now - or they may, back there," and he nodded to indicate the air headquarters he and Tom had left. "You know we're going to be under Pershing soon," he added.

"So you wrote me," said Bessie. "I'm glad, though it's all in the same good cause. Well, as I was saying, Nellie came to our hospital-I call it ours though I have such a small part in it," she interjected. "She was introduced to us as an American, and of course we made friends at once."

"No one could help making friends with Bessie and her

mother!" exclaimed Nellie.

"Don't flatter us too much," warned Bessie. "Now please don't interrupt any more. As I say, Nellie came to us to do her share in helping care for the wounded, and, as mother and I found she had settled on no regular place in Paris, we asked her to share our rooms. Then we got to talking, and of course I found she had met you two boys in her search for her brother. After that we were better friends than ever."

"Glad to know it," said Tom. "There's nothing like having friends. I hadn't any notion that I'd meet any when I started out with him tonight," and he motioned to Jack.

"Well, I like that!" cried Bessie in feigned indignation. "I like to know how you class my mother and me?" and she looked at Tom.

"Oh, - er - well, of course - you and your mother, and Jack. But he and you -"

"Better swim out before you get into deep water," advised Jack quickly, and he nudged Tom with his foot.

Then the boys had to tell about their final experiences before leaving the Lafayette Escadrille with which many trying, as well as many happy, hours were associated, and the girls told of their adventures, which were not altogether tame.

Since Mrs. Gleason had been freed from the plotting of the spy, Potzfeldt, she had lived a happy life - that is as happy as one could amid the scenes of war and its attendant horrors. She and Bessie were throwing themselves heart and soul into the immortal work of the Red Cross, and now Nellie bad joined them.

"It's the only way I can stop thinking about poor Harry," she said with a sigh. "Oh, if I could only hear some good news about him, that I might send it to the folks at home. Do you think it will ever come - the good news, I mean?" she asked wistfully of Tom.

"All we can do is to hope," he said. He knew better than to buoy up false hopes, for he had seen too much of the terrible side of war. In his heart he knew that there was but little chance for Harry Leroy, after the latter's aeroplane had been shot down behind the German lines. Yet there was that one, slender hope to which all of us cling when it seems that everything else is lost.

"He may be a prisoner, and, in that case, there is a chance," said Tom, while Jack and Bessie were conversing on the other side of the room.

"You mean a chance to escape?"

"Hardly that, though it has been done. A few aviators have got away from German prison camps. But it's only one chance in many thousand. No, what I meant was that - well, it's too small and slim a chance to talk about, I'm afraid."

"Oh, no!" she hastened to assure him. "Do tell me! No chance is too small. What do you mean?"

"Well, sometimes rescues have been made," went on Tom. "They are even more rare than escapes, but they have been done. I was thinking that perhaps after Jack and I get in with Pershing's boys we might be in some big raid on the Hun lines, and then, if we could get any information as to your brother's whereabouts, we might plan to rescue him."

"Oh, do you think you could?"

"I certainly can and will try!" exclaimed Tom, earnestly.

"Oh, will you? Oh, I can't thank you enough!" and she clasped his hand in both hers and Tom blushed deeply.

"Please don't count too much on it," Tom warned Nellie. "It's a desperate chance at best, but it's the only one I can see that we can take. First of all, though, we've got to get some word as to where Harry is."

"How can you do that?"

"Some of the Hun airmen are almost human, that is compared to the other Boche fighters. They may drop a cap of Harry's or a glove, or something," and Tom told of the practice in such cases.

"Oh, if they only will!" sighed Nellie. "But it is almost too much to hope."

And so they talked until late in the evening, when the time came for Nellie, Bessie and her mother to report back for their Red Cross work. The boys returned to their hotel, promising to write often and to see their friends at the next opportunity.

"I won't forget!" said Tom, on parting from Nellie.

"Forget what?" asked Jack, as they were going down the street together.

"I'm going to do my best to rescue her brother," said Tom, in a low voice.

"Good! I'm with you!" declared Jack.

The stay of the two boys in Paris was all too short, but they were anxious to get back to their work. They wanted to be fighting under their own flag. Not that they had not been doing all they could for liberty, but it was different, being with their own countrymen. And so, when their leaves of absence were up, they took the train that was to drop them at the place assigned, where the newly arrived Americans were beginning their training.

"The American front!" cried Tom, as he and Jack reached the headquarters of General Pershing and his associate officers. "The American front at last!"

"And it's the happiest day of my life that I can fight on it!" cried Jack.

CHAPTER VIII

A BATTLE IN THE AIR

Strictly speaking there was at that time no American front. That did not come until later, for the American soldiers, as was proper, were brigaded with the French and British, to enable our troops, who were unused to European war conditions, to become acquainted with the needful measures to meet and overcome the brutality of the Huns.

But even with this brigading of the United States' troops with the seasoned veterans, which, in plain language, meant a mingling of the two forces, there was much that was strictly American among the new arrivals.

Not only were the khaki-clad soldiers real Americans to the backbone, but their equipment and the supplies that had come over with them in the transports were such as might be seen at any army camp in this country, as distinguished from a French or a British camp.

"Well, the boys are here all right," remarked Jack, as he and Tom made their way toward the headquarters at which they were to report.

"Yes, and it makes me feel good to see them!" said Tom. "This is the beginning of the end of Kaiserism, if I'm any judge."

"Oh, it isn't going to be so easy as all that," returned Jack.

"We'll see some hard fighting. Germany isn't licked yet by any means; but those, are the boys that can bring the thing to a finish," and he pointed to a company of the lean, stem, brown figures that were swinging along with characteristic stride.

The place at which Tom and Jack had been ordered to report was an interior city of France, not far from the port at which the first transport from America had arrived. A first glance at the scenes on every hand would have given a person not familiar with war a belief that hopeless confusion existed. Wagons, carts, mule teams and motor trucks-"lorries," the English call them - were dashing to and fro. Men were marching, countermarching, unloading some vehicles, loading others. Soldiers were being marched into the interior to be billeted, others were being directed to their respective French or English units. Officers were shouting commands, and privates were carrying them out to the best of their ability.

But though it all seemed chaos, out of it order was coming. There was a system, though a civilian would not have understood it.

"Well, let's find out where we're at," suggested Torn, to his chum.

"Right O, my pickled grapefruit!" agreed Jack with a laugh. "Let's get into the game."

They were about to ask their direction from a non-commissioned officer who was directing a squad of men in the unloading of a truck which seemed filled with canned goods, when some one said:

"There goes Black Jack now!"

The two air service boys looked, and saw, passing along not far away, a tall man, faultlessly attired, who looked "every inch a soldier," and whose square jaw was indicative of his fighting qualities, if the rest of his face had not been.

"Is that General Pershing?" asked Tom, in a low voice of the non-commissioned officer.

"That's who he is, buddy," was the smiling answer. "The best man in the world for the job, too. Come on there now, you with the red hair. This isn't a croquet game. Lay into those cases, and get 'em off some time before New Year's. We want to have our Christmas dinner in Berlin, remember!"

"So that's Pershing," commented Jack, as he looked at the American commander, who, with his staff officers, was on a trip of inspection. "Well, he suits me all right!"

"The next thing for us to do is to find out if we suit him," remarked Tom. "Wonder if he knows we're here?"

"I don't even believe he knows we're alive!" exclaimed Jack, for the moment taking Tom's joke quite seriously.

As General Pershing passed on, receiving and returning many salutes, Tom and Jack made their inquiries, learned where they were to report, and went on their way, longing for the time when they could get into action with the American troops.

"Oh, so you're the two aviators from the Lafayette Escadrille," commented the commanding officer, or the C. O., of the newly formed American squadron, as Tom and Jack, drawing themselves up as straight as they could, saluted when he looked over their papers and their log books. These last are the personal records of aviators in which they note the details of each flight made. They are official documents, but when a birdman is honorably discharged he may take his log book with him.

"We were told to report to you, sir," said Tom.

"Yes. And I'm glad to see you. We're going to establish a purely American air force, but as yet it is in its infancy. I need some experienced fliers, and I'm glad you're going to be with us. Of course I have a number who have made good records over there," and he nodded to indicate the United States, "But they haven't been under fire yet, and I understand you have."

"Some," admitted Jack, modestly enough.

"Good! Well, I'm to have some more of our own boys, who are to be transferred from the French forces, and some from the Royal Flying Corps, so with that as a start I guess we can build up an air service that will make Fritz step lively. But we've got to go slow. One thing I'm sorry for is that we haven't, as yet, any American planes. We'll have to depend on the French and English for them, as we have to, at first, for our artillery and shells."

"We can fly French or British planes," remarked Tom.

And, as my old readers know, the air service boys had had experience with a number of different models.

"We can fly a Gotha if we have to," said Jack. "One came down back of our lines last month, and we patched it up and flew it for practice."

"I hope you can get some more of that practice," said the commanding officer with a smile.

"But, now that you're here, I'll swear you in and see what the orders are regarding you. I'm afraid there won't be much fighting for you at first - that is strictly as Americans. I understand our air front, if I may use that term, will have to grow out of a nucleus of French and English fighters."

"That's all right, as long as we get the right start," commented Tom.

It was necessary to swear the boys into the service of the United States, even though they were natives of it; since, on entering the Lafayette Escadrille, they had been obliged to swear allegiance to France. But this was a matter of routine where the Allies were concerned, and soon Tom and Jack were back again where they longed to be - enrolled among the distinctive fighters of their own country.

They were assigned to barracks, and found themselves among some other airmen, many of whom were student fliers from the various aviation camps of the United States. Few of these youths had had much practice, though some had been to the Canadian schools. And none of them had, as yet, fought an enemy in the air.

To aid and instruct them, however, were such fighters as Tom and Jack, and some even more experienced from the French, Italian and British camps, who had been detailed to help out the United States in the emergency.

The next few weeks was an instruction and reconstruction period, with Tom and Jack often filling the roles of teachers. They found their pupils apt, eager and willing, however, and among them they discovered some excellent material. As the commanding officer of the new American air forces had said, the planes used were all of English or French make. It was too early in the war for America to have sent any over equipped with the Liberty motor, though production was under way.

After this period had passed, Tom and Jack, with a squadron of other birdmen were sent to a certain section of the front held largely by American troops, supported by veteran French and British regiments.

It was the first wholly American aircraft camp established since the beginning of the World War, and it was not even yet as wholly American as it was destined to be later, for the aviators were, as regards veterans, largely French and English. Torn and Jack were, in point of service, the ranking American fliers for a time.

There had been several sharp engagements across No Man's

Land between the mingled French, British and French forces and the Huns, and honors were on the side of the former. There had been one or two combats in the air, in which Tom and Jack had taken part, when one day word came from an observation balloon on the American side that a flock of German aircraft was on the way from a camp located a few miles within the Boche lines.

There was a harried consultation of the officers, and then orders were given for a half score of the Allied machines to get ready. Two veteran French aces were to be in command, with Tom and Jack as helpers, and some of the American aviators were to go into the battle of the air for the first time.

"The Huns are evidently going to try to bomb some of our ammunition dumps behind our lines,"' said one officer, speaking to Tom. "It's up to you boys to drive 'em back."

"We'll try, sir," was the answer. "We owe the Huns something we haven't been able to pay off as yet."

Tom referred to the loss of Harry Leroy. So far no word had been received from him, either directly or through the German aviators, as to whether he was dead or a prisoner. Letters had passed between Bessie and Nellie and Jack and Tom, and the sister of the missing youth begged for news.

But there was none to give her.

"Unless we get some to-day," observed Tom as he and his chum hurried toward the hangars where their machines were being made ready for them.

"Get news to-day? What makes you think we shall?" asked Jack.

"Well, we might bring down a Fritzie or two who'd know something about poor Harry," was the answer. "You never can tell."

"No, that's so," agreed Jack. "Well, here's hoping we'll have luck."

By this time there was great excitement in the American aviation headquarters. Word of the oncoming Hun planes had spread, and not a flier of Pershing's forces but was eager to get into his plane and go aloft to give battle. But only the best were selected, and if there were heart-burnings of disappointment it could not be helped.

Two classes of planes were to be used, the single seaters for the aces, who fought alone, and the double craft, each one of which carried a pilot and an observer. In the latter cases the observers were the new men, who had yet to receive their baptism of fire above the clouds.

Tom and Jack were each detailed to take up one of the new men, and the air service boys were glad to find that, assigned to each of them, was the very man he would have picked had he had his choice. They were eager, intrepid lads, anxious to do their share in the great adventure.

Quickly the machines were made ready, and quickly the fighters climbed into them. The roar of the motors was heard all over the aerodrome, and soon the machines began to mount. Up and up they climbed, and none too soon, for on reaching elevations averaging ten thousand feet, there was seen, over the German lines, a flock of the Hun planes led by two or three machines painted a bright red. These were some of the machines that had belonged to the celebrated "flying circus," organized by a daring Hun aviator and ace who was killed after he had inflicted great damage and loss on the Allied service. He and his men had their machines painted red, perhaps on the theory that they would thus inspire terror. These were some of the former members of the circus," it was evident.

"It's going to be a real fight!" cried Tom, as he headed his machine toward one of the red craft. Whether the green man Tom was taking up relished this or not, knowing, as he must, the reputation of these red aviators, Tom did not stop to consider.

Then, as the two hostile air fleets approached, there began a battle of the clouds - a conflict destined to end fatally for more than one aviator.

CHAPTER IX

THE FALLING GLOVE

Numerically the Hun planes, were superior to the American fleet of airships that quickly rose to oppose them. That probably accounted for fact that the Germans did not turn tail and scurry back beyond the protection of their own anti-aircraft guns and batteries. For it was seldom, if ever, they went into a fight when the odds were against them.

On came the Fokkers and Gothas, the black iron crosses painted on the wings of the machines standing out in bold relief in the clear air. The sun glinted on the red craft which were in the lead, and besides Tom, who headed for one of these, a French ace darted down from a height to engage the red planes.

"See if you can plug him when I put you near enough!" cried Tom to his observer, who had the reputation of being a good shot with the Lewis gun. Practice with the machine weapons in aeroplanes had been going on, for some time among the new American aviators. "Let him have a good dose!" cried Tom. "If you miss him, then I'll try!"

Of course Tom had to shut off the engine when he said this, as no voice could have been heard above the roaring of the powerful motor. But when he had given his companion these instructions and had ascertained, by a glance over his shoulder, that the lad understood for he nodded his head, Tom again turned on the gasoline, and the propeller, that had been revolving by momentum and because of the pressure of air against it, took up its speed again.

Straight for the red machine rushed Tom, and a quick glance told him that his companion was ready with the gun. The weapon to be worked by the latter was mounted so that it could be aimed independently of the aeroplane. Tom also had a gun in front of him, but it was fixed and could be aimed only by pointing the whole craft. Once this was done Tom could operate the weapon with one hand, steering with the other, and, at times, with his feet and knees.

There came several sharp pops near Tom's head, and he knew these were machine bullets from the Hun aviator's gun, breaking through the tightly stretched linen fabric of the wings of his own plane.

"Let him have it before he plugs us!" cried Tom to his companion, though of course the latter could not hear a word. An instant later Tom heard the Lewis gun behind him firing, and he saw several tracer bullets strike the Hun machine. But they were not near the aviator himself, and did no material damage.

"Guess he's too nervous to shoot straight," reasoned Tom. "I'll have to try my own gun," he decided.

Tom noticed that the Hun was climbing up, trying to get into a position above the American plane, which is always an advantage. And the air service boy knew he must not let this happen. Quickly he shifted the rudder and began to climb himself. But he was at a disadvantage as his machine carried double, while the red plane had only one man in it, an ace beyond a doubt.

"I've got to get him now or never!" thought Tom. Once more he shifted his direction, and then, as he had his gun aimed just where he wanted it, he pressed the lever and a burst of bullets shot out and fairly riddled the red plane. It seemed to stop for an instant in the air, and then, quivering, turned and went down in a nose dive, spinning around.

"No fake about that!" mused Tom, as he leaned over and looked down from the height. "He's done for I"

And so, the Hun was, for he crashed to the ground behind the American lines. The incident did not affect Tom Raymond greatly. It was not his first killing. But when he, glanced back toward his companion, he saw that the other was shrinking back as if in horror.

"He'll get over that soon enough. All he has to do is to think of what the Huns have done - crucifying men and babies - to make his heart hard," thought Tom.

Whether his companion did this or not, did not disclose itself, but the fact remains that when Tom flew off to engage another Hun machine the lad back of him rose to the occasion and shot so well that Fritz veered off and flew back over his own lines, wounded and with his craft barely able to fly.

Not all the American machines fared as well as this, however. Jack was in poor luck. The first burst of bullets from the German he engaged punctured his gasoline tank, and he was obliged to coast back to his own aerodrome to get another machine, if possible. He was also hit once in the leg, the wound being painful though not dangerous. He received first aid treatment and wanted to get back into the fight, but this was not allowed, and he had to watch the battle from the ground.

The fight was fast and stubborn, and in the end the American forces won, for at a signal from the remaining red plane, which seemed to bear a charmed existence, as it did not appear to be hit, the others remaining of the Hun forces, turned tail and scooted back to safety.

But they had left a toll of five machines sent crashing to earth, four of them each containing two men. The leading French ace was killed, a severe loss to the Allied forces, and three of the American machines were damaged and their operators severely wounded, though with a chance of recovery. By American machines is meant those assigned for use to Pershing's forces, though the craft used up to that time were of French or English make. The real American machines came into use a little later.

"Well, I think we can call it one to our credit," said Tom, as he rejoined Jack after the battle.

"Yes. But you had all the luck!" complained his chum. "It went against me, and the lad I took up. It - "

"Never mind; it'll be your turn next," replied Tom, consolingly.

And so the new American aviators received their baptism of fire, and, to their credit, longed for more.

More credit was really due the American forces than would be indicated by the mere citation of the losses inflicted on the German side in this first air battle. For many of the American fighters were "green," while not one of the Huns, as was learned later, but what had several Allied machines to his score. And so there was rejoicing in General Pershing's camp, even though it was mingled with sorrow at the losses inflicted.

Busy days followed, Tom and Jack were in the air much of the time. And when they were not flying they were delivering talks to new students, who were constantly arriving. They found time once to run into Paris on their day of leave, to see Bessie and Nellie, and they went on a little picnic together, which was as jolly as such an affair could be in the midst of the terrible war. Nellie had received no word of her missing brother, and Jack and Tom had no encouragement for her.

Then came more hard work at camp, and another battle of the air in which the American forces more than equaled matters, for they fairly demolished a German plane squadron, sending ten of the machines crashing to earth and the others back over the Hun lines, more or less damaged. That was a great day. And, as a sort of reward for their work, Tom and Jack were given three days' leave. At first they thought to spend them in Paris, but, learning that neither Bessie nor her mother nor Nellie could leave their Red Cross work to join them, the two lads made other arrangements.

"Let's go back and see the fellows in the Lafayette Escadrille," suggested Tom.

"All right," agreed Jack.

And thither they went.

That they were welcomed need not be said. It was comparatively quiet on this sector just then, though there had, a few days before, been a great battle with victory perching on the Allied banners. The air conflicts, too, had been desperate, and many a brave man of the French, English or American fliers had met his death. But toll had been taken of the Boches - ample toll, too.

The first inquiry Tom and Jack had made on their arrival at their former aerodrome had been for news of Harry Leroy, but none had been received.

It was when Tom and Jack were about to conclude their visit to their former comrades of the air that an incident occurred which made a great change in their lives. One sunny afternoon there suddenly appeared, a mere speck in the blue, a single aeroplane.

"Some one of your men must have gone a long way over Heinie's lines," remarked Jack to one of the French officers.

"He is not one of our men. Either they were all back long ago or they will not come back until after the war - if ever. That is a Hun machine."

"What is he doing - challenging to single combat?" asked Tom, as the lone plane came on steadily.

"No," answered the officer, after a look through his glasses. "I think he brings some messages. We sent some to the Germans yesterday, and I think this is a return courtesy. We will wait and see."

Nearer and nearer came the German plane. Soon it was circling around the French camp. Hundreds came out to watch, for now the object of the lone aviator was apparent. He contemplated no raid. It was to drop news of captured, or dead, Allied airmen.

Then, as Tom, and the others watched, a little package was seen to fall from the hovering aeroplane. It landed on the roof of one of the hangars, bounced off and was picked up by an orderly, who presented it to the commanding officer.

Quickly and eagerly it was opened. It contained some personal belongings of Allied airmen who had been missing for the past week. Some of them, the message from the German lines said, had been killed by their falls after being shot down, and it was stated that they had been decently buried. Others were wounded and in hospitals.

"No word from Harry," said Tom, sadly, as the last of the relics from the dead and the living were gone over.

"Well, I guess we may as well give him up," added Jack. "But we can avenge him. That's all we have left, now."

"Yes," agreed Tom. "If we only - ?"

A cry from some of those watching the German plane

interrupted him. The two air service boys looked up. Another small object was falling. It landed with a thud, almost at the feet of Tom and Jack, and the latter picked it up.

It was an aviator's glove; and as Jack held it up a note dropped out. Quickly it was read, and the import of it was given to all in a simultaneous shout of joy from Tom and Jack.

"It's word from Harry Leroy! Word from Harry at last!"

CHAPTER X

STUNTS

Truly enough, word had come from the missing aviator, or, if not directly from him, at least from his captors. The German airmen, falling in with the chivalry which had been initiated by the French and English, and later followed by the Americans, had seen fit to inform the comrades of the captured man of his whereabouts.

"Where is he? What happened to him?" asked several, as all crowded around Tom and Jack to hear the news.

Jack, reading the note, told them. The missive was written in very good English, though in a German hand. It stated that Harry Leroy had been shot down in his plane while over the German lines, and had fallen in a lonely spot, wounded.

The wound was not serious, it was stated, and the prisoner was doing as well as could be expected, but he would remain in the hands of his captors until the end of the war. The reason his whereabouts was not mentioned before was that the Germans did not know they had one of the Allied aviators in their midst.

Leroy had not only fallen in a lonely spot, but he was made unconscious by his fall and injuries, and when he recovered he was lying near his almost demolished plane.

He managed to get out his log book and other confidential papers, and set fire to them and the plane with the gasoline that still remained in the tank. He destroyed them so they might not fall into the hands of the Germans, a fate he knew would be his own shortly.

But Harry Leroy was not doomed to instant capture. The blaze caused by his burning aeroplane attracted the attention of a peasant, who had not been deported when the enemy overran his country, for the young aviator had fallen in a spot well back of the front lines. This French peasant took Harry to his little farm and hid him in the barn. There the man, his wife, and his granddaughters, looked after the injured aviator, feeding him and binding up his hurts. It was a great risk they took, and Harry Leroy knew it as well as they. But for nearly two weeks he remained hidden, and this probably saved his life, for he got better treatment at the farmhouse than he would, as an enemy, have received in a German hospital.

But such good luck could not last. Suspicion that Americans were hidden in the Frenchman's barn began to spread through the country, and rather than bring discovery on his friends, Leroy left the barn one night.

He had a desperate hope that he might reach his own lines, as he was now pretty well recovered from his 'Injuries, but it was not to be. He was captured by a German patrol. But by his quick action Harry Leroy had removed suspicion from the farmer, which was exactly what he wished to do.

The Germans, rejoicing over their capture, took the young aviator to the nearest prison camp, and there he was put in custody, together with some unfortunate French and English. The tide of war had turned against Harry Leroy.

So it came about that, some time after he had been posted as missing and when it was surely thought that he was dead, Harry Leroy was found to be among the living, though a prisoner.

"This will be great news for his sister!" exclaimed Jack, as the note dropped by the German airman was read over and over again.

"Yes, she'll be delighted," agreed Tom. "We must hurry back and tell her."

"And that isn't all," went on Jack. "We must try to figure out a way to rescue Harry."

"You can't do that," declared a French ace, one with whom the air service boys had often flown.

"Why not?" asked Tom.

"It's out of the question," was the answer. "There has never been a rescue yet from behind the German lines. Or, if there has been, it's like a blue moon."

"Well, we can try," declared Jack, and Tom nodded his head in agreement.

"Don't count too much on it," added another of their friends. "Harry may not even be where this note says he is."

"Do you mean that the Germans would say what isn't so?" asked Tom.

"Of course! Naturally!" was the answer. "But even if they did not in this case, even if they have truly said where Leroy is, he may be moved at any time - sent to some other prison, or made to work in the mines or at perhaps something far worse."

Tom and Jack realized that this might be so, and they felt that there was no easy task ahead of them in trying to rescue their chum from the hands of the Germans. But they were not youths who gave up easily.

"May we keep this note?" asked Tom, as he and Jack got ready to depart. Having fallen on the camp of the escadrille with which they were formerly quartered, it was, strictly speaking, the property of the airmen there. But having been told how much the sister of the prisoner would appreciate it, the commanding officer gave permission for Tom and Jack to take the glove and note with them.

"Let us know if you rescue him, Comrades!" called the Frenchmen to the two lads, as they started back for their own camp.

"We will," was the answer.

Nellie Leroy's joy in the news that her brother was alive was tempered by the fact that he was a German prisoner.

"But we're going to get him!" declared Tom even though he realized, as he said it, that it with almost a forlorn hope.

"You are so good," murmured the girl.

Jack and Tom spent a few happy hours in Paris, with Nellie and Bessie - the last of their leave - and then, bidding the girls and Mrs. Gleason farewell, they reported back to the American aerodrome, where the young airmen were cordially welcomed.

There they found much to do, and events followed one another so rapidly at this stage of the World War that Tom and Jack, after their return, had little time for anything but flying and teaching others what they knew of air work. They had no opportunity to do anything toward the rescue of Harry Leroy; and, indeed, they were at a loss how to proceed. They were just hoping that something would transpire to give them a starting point.

"We'll have to leave it to luck for a while," said Torn.

"Or fate," added Jack.

"Well, fate plays no small part in an airman's life," returned Tom. "While we are no more superstitions than any other soldiers, yet there are few airmen who do not carry some sort of mascot or good-luck piece. You know that, Jack."

And even the casual reader of the exploits of the aviators must have been impressed with the fact that often the merest incident - or accident is responsible for life or death.

Death often passes within hair's breadth of the intrepid fliers, and some of them do not know it until after they have made a landing and have seen the bullet holes in their machine - holes that indicate how close the missiles have passed to them.

So, in a way, both Tom and Jack believed in luck, and they both believed that this same luck might point out to them a way of rescuing Harry Leroy.

Meanwhile they were kept busy. After the big battle in the air matters were quiet for a time on their sector of the front. The arrival of new fliers from America made it necessary to instruct them, and to this Tom, Jack and other veterans were detailed.

Then began a series of what Jack called "stunts." In order to inspire the new pupils with confidence, the older flying men – not always older in years - would go aloft in their single planes and do all sorts of trick flying. Some of the pupils - the more daring, of course - wished to imitate these, but of course they were not allowed.

The pupils were first allowed merely to go with an experienced man. This, of course, they had done at the flying schools in the United States, and had flown alone. But they had to start all over again when on French soil, for here they were exposed, any time, to an attack from a Hun plane.

After they had, it was thought, got sufficient experience to undertake these trick features by themselves, they were allowed to make trial flights, but not over the enemy lines.

Tom and Jack gave the best that was in them to these enthusiastic pupils, and there was much good material.

"What are you going to do to-day, Jack?" asked Tom one morning, as they went out after breakfast to get into their "busses," as they dubbed their machines.

"Oh, got orders to do some spiral and somersault stunts for the benefit of some huns." ("Hun," used in this connection, not referring to the Germans. "Hun" is the slang term for student aviators, tacked on them by more experienced fliers.)

"Same here. Good little bunch of huns in camp now."

Tom nodded in agreement, and the two were soon preparing to climb aloft.

With a watching group of eager young men on the ground below, in company with an instructor who would point out the way certain feats were done, Torn and Jack began climbing. Presently they were fairly tumbling about like pigeons, seeming to fall, but quickly straightening out on a level keel and coming to the ground almost as lightly as feathers.

"A good landing is essential if one would become a good airman," stated the instructor. "In fact I may say it is the hardest half of the game. For it is comparatively easy to leave the earth. It is the coining back that is difficult, like the Irishman who said it wasn't the fall that hurts, it was the stopping."

"Give 'em a bit of zooming now," the instructor said to Tom and Jack. "The boys may have to use that any time they're up and a Boche comes at them."

"Zooming," he went on to the pupils, "is rising and falling in a series of abrupt curves like those in a roller-coaster railway. It is a very useful stunt to be master of, for it enables one to rise quickly when confronting a field barrier, or to get out of range of a Hun machine gun."

Tom undertook this feature of the instruction, as Jack signaled that his aeroplane was out of gasoline, and soon the former was rolling across the aviation field, seemingly straight toward a row of tall trees.

"He'll hit 'em sure!" cried one student.

"Watch him," ordered the instructor.

With a quick pull on the lever that controlled the rudder, Tom sent himself aloft, but not before a curious thing happened.

On the ground where it had been dropped was a tunic, or airman's fur-lined jacket. As Tom's machine "zoomed," the tail skid caught this jacket and took it aloft.

Tom did not seem to be aware of this, though he must have felt that his machine was a bit sluggish in the climbs. However, he went through with his performance, doing some beautiful "zooming," and then, as he was flying high and getting ready to do a spiral nose dive, the tunic detached itself from his skid and fell.

Just at this moment Jack came out from the hangar and, looking aloft and noting Tom's machine, saw the falling jacket. His heart turned sick and faint, for, unaware of what had happened, he thought his chum had tumbled out while at a great height. For the tunic, turning over and over as it sailed earthward, did resemble a falling body.

"Oh, Tom! Tom! How did it happen?" murmured Jack.

The others, laughing, told him that it was nothing serious, but Jack looked a bit worried until the empty jacket fell on the grass and, a little later, Tom himself came down smiling from aloft, all unaware of the excitement he had caused.

CHAPTER XI

OVER THE LINES

"Well, I guess we stay downstairs, to-day," remarked Tom to Jack, the day following their exhibition flights for the benefit of the air students.

"Yes, it doesn't look very promising," returned his chum.

Jack looked aloft where the sky - or what took its place - was represented by a gray mist that seemed ready to drip water at any moment. It was a day of "low visibility," and one when air work was almost totally suspended. This applied to the enemy as well as to the Yankees. For even though it is feasible to go up in an aeroplane in fog, or even rain or snow, it is not always safe to come down again in like conditions.

There is nothing worse than rain, snow or fog for clouding an aviator's goggles, making it impossible for him to see more than a plane's length ahead, if, indeed, he can see that far. Then, too, little, if anything, can be accomplished by going aloft in a storm or fog. No observations of any account can be made, and the aviator, once he gets aloft, is as likely to come down behind the German lines as he is to descend safely within his own.

That being the case, Tom and Jack, in common with their comrades of the air, had a vacation period. Some of them obtained leave and went to the nearest town, while some put in their time going over their guns and glasses and equipment and machines.

Jack and Tom elected to do the latter. There was one very fast and powerful Spad which they often used together, taking turns at piloting it and acting as observer. They thought they might have a chance soon to go over the German lines in this, their favorite craft, so they decided to put in their spare time seeing that it was in perfect shape, and that the two machine guns were ready for action when needed.

"'Would you rather do this than fly, Jack?" asked Tom, as they went over, in detail, each part of the powerful Spad.

"I should say not! But, after all, one is just as important as the other. I hope we get a good day to-morrow. I'd like to do something toward seeing if we can't get Harry out of the Boche's clutches," and he nodded in the direction of the German lines.

"'Tisn't going to be easy doing that," remarked Tom. "I'd ask nothing better than to have a hand in getting him away, but I haven't yet been able to figure out a shadow of a plan. Have you?"

"The only thing, I can think of is to organize a big raid on the section where he's held - I mean somewhere near the German prison - and if we bombed the place enough, and created enough excitement, some of us might land and get Harry and any others that might be with him."

Tom shook his head.

"That'd be a pretty risky way of doing it," he said.

"Can you think of a better?" Jack demanded quickly.

"Not off hand," came the reply. "We've got to stew over it a bit. One thing's sure - we've got to get Harry out, or his sister never will feel like going back home and facing the folks."

"That's right!" agreed Jack. "We've got a double motive for this. But I'm afraid it's going to be too hard."

"That's what we thought when we rescued Mrs. Gleason from the old castle where Potzfeldt had her caged," retorted Tom. "But you made out all right."

"Yes; thanks to your help."

"Well, we'll both work together again," declared Tom. "And now let's try this Lewis gun. The last time we were up it jammed on me, and yet it worked all right on the ground." So they tested the guns, looked to the motor, and in general made ready for a flight when the weather should clear.

This happened two days later, when the fog and mist were blown away and the blue sky could be seen. In the interim the artillery and infantry on both sides had not been idle, and there had been some desperate engagements, with the brigaded American troops making a new name for themselves.

"I guess there'll be something doing to-day," remarked Tom, as he and Jack tumbled out of bed at the usual early hour. "Clear as a bell," he announced, after a glance from the window. "Shouldn't wonder but what we went over their lines to-day."

"And I suppose, by the same token, they'll be coining over ours," and Jack nodded to indicate the Germans.

"Let 'em come!" exclaimed Tom. "It takes two sides to make a fight, and that's what we're here for."

Hardly had the two air service boys finished their breakfast, than an orderly came to tell them the commanding officer wanted them to report to him. They hurried across the aviation ground, toward the headquarters building, noting on the way that there were signs of unusual activity among the newer members of the American air forces, as well as among the French and British veterans.

"Must be going to make a raid," observed Jack.

"Something like that - yes," assented Tom.

"Hope we're in on it, and the commanding officer doesn't have us take some huns up to show 'em what makes the wheels go around," went on Jack. "Of course that's part of the game, but we've done our share."

However, they need have felt no fear, for when they stood before the commanding officer, saluting, they quickly learned that they were to go on a special mission that day - in fact as soon as they could get ready.

"I want you two to see if you can discover a battery of small guns that have been playing havoc with our men," he said, as he looked up from a table covered with maps. "They're located somewhere along this front, but they're so well camouflaged that no one has yet been able to discover them.

"I want you boys to see if you can turn the trick. The guns have killed a lot of our men, as well as the French and English. We've tried to rush the emplacement, but we can't get a line on where it is for it's well hidden. I asked permission of the British commanding general to send up two American scouts, and he mentioned you boys. Get your orders from the major, and good luck to you."

"Do you want us to go together or separately?" asked Tom.

"Together - in a double plane. I might say that we are going to try a raid on a big scale over the enemy's lines, and you two will thus have a better chance to carry out your observations unmolested. The Hun planes will have their hands full attending to our fighters, and they may not attack a single plane off by itself. We'll try to draw them away from you.

"At the same time I might point out that there is nothing sure in this, and that you may have to fight also," concluded the commanding officer, as he waved a dismissal.

"Oh, were ready for anything," announced Tom. And as he and Jack got outside he clapped his chum on the back, crying: "That's the stuff! Good old C.O. to send us! That's what we've been looking for! Maybe we'll have time to drop down and shoot some of the Huns that are guarding Harry."

"No chance of that - forget it now," urged Jack. "We'll clean up this location trick first, and then think of a plan to get Harry away. It sounds hard to say it, but it's all we can do. Orders are orders."

They were glad they had made ready the speedy Spad plane, for it was in this that they would try to locate the hidden battery, and, having received detailed instructions from the major in command, the two lads climbed into their air plane and started off.

The day was clear and bright, just the sort for aeroplane activity; and it was evident there would be plenty of it, since, even as they began climbing, Tom and Jack saw planes from their own aerodrome skirting ahead of and behind them, while, in the distance and over German-held territory, were Fokkers and Gothas with the iron cross conspicuously painted on each.

Tom and Jack had been given a map of the front, their own and the German lines being shown, and the probable location of the hidden Hun battery marked. This they now studied as they started over the front, Jack being in front, while Tom sat behind him, to work the swivel Lewis gun.

Their Spad machine was one that could be controlled from either seat, so that if one rider was disabled the other could take charge. There were two guns, one fixed and the other movable, and a good supply of ammunition.

"Well, I guess there'll be some fighting to-day," observed Tom, as Jack shut off the motor for a moment, to see if it would respond readily when the throttle was opened again. "They're closing in from both sides."

And indeed the Allied planes were sailing forth to meet a squadron of the enemy. But none of the Hun craft seemed to pay any attention to Tom and Jack. Steadily they flew on until an exclamation from Jack caused Tom to look down. He noted that they were over the German lines, and headed for the probable location of the battery that had been such a thorn in the side of the Allies.

CHAPTER XII

A PERFECT SHOT

The plane in which Tom and Jack had gone aloft to make observations which, it was hoped, would result in the discovery of the hidden battery, was a special machine. While very powerful and swift and equipped for air-fighting, it was also one that had been used by one of the French photographers and his pilot. The photographer, was a daring man, and had, not long before, gone to his death in fighting three Hun planes. But he had peculiar ideas regarding his car, and under his orders it had been fitted with a glass floor in the two cockpits, or what corresponded to them.

Thus he and his pilot could look down and observe the nature of the enemy country over which they were traveling without having to lean over, not always a safe act where anti-aircraft guns below are shooting up shrapnel.

So as Torn and Jack flew on and on, over the enemy's first and succeeding line trenches, they looked down through the glass windows in the plane to make their observations. There was a camera attached to the plane, and though they could each make use of it, but they were not skilled in this work.

It was impossible for them to talk to one another now, as Jack had the motor going almost full speed, and the noise it made was deafening, or it would have been except for the warm, fur hoods that covered the ears of the fliers. They were warmly dressed for they did not know how high they might ascend, and it is always cold up above, no matter how hot it is on the earth.

Up and up they climbed, and then they flew on and over the enemy lines, keeping close lookout for anything unusual below that would indicate the presence of the battery. Behind them, and off to one side, a fierce aerial battle was going on.

Tom and Jack were eager to get into this and do their share. But they had orders to make their observations, and they dared not 'refuse. They could tell by looking back every now and then that the affair was going well for the Allies, including some of the American airmen, even if the Huns outnumbered them.

Back and forth over the German lines swept the glass-bottomed Spad, and at a certain point Tom, who was looking down, uttered an exclamation. Of course Jack could not hear, but he could feel the punch in the back his chum administered a moment later.

Jack turned his head, and saw his chum eagerly pointing downward. A moment later he motioned over his left shoulder, pointing backward, as though they had just passed over something which would warrant a second inspection.

Jack swung the machine about in a big circle, banking sharply, and then, as he passed over the ground covered a little while before, he, too, looked down, and with sharper glance than he had used at first.

What he saw was the ruins of a small French chateau. It had been under heavy fire from the Allied guns, for it had sheltered a German machine gun nest, and some accurate shooting on the part of the American gunners had demolished it a day or so before.

But what attracted the attention of Tom and Jack was that

whereas the chateau before the bombardment had stood on a little hill without a tree near it, now there was a miniature forest surrounding it. It was as though trees and bushes had sprung up in the night. As soon as he had seen this, Jack turned to Tom, nodded comprehendingly, and at once started back over the American lines. They had no easy time reaching them, for by this time the fleet of Hun planes had been defeated by the Allies, and had turned tail to run for safety - that is what were left of them, several having been shot down, and at no small cost to the French, English and American forces.

But the defeat of their airmen seemed to anger the Germans, and they opened up with their antiaircraft batteries on the machine in which Tom and Jack were flying homeward. "Woolly bears" and "flaming onions," as well as shrapnel, was used against them, and they were in considerable danger. Jack had to "zoom" several times to get out of reach of the shells.

They finally reached their aerodrome, however, and as soon as they had landed and their plane was taken in charge by the mechanics the two lads hurried to the commanding officer.

"Well?" he asked sharply, as they saluted. "Did you discover anything?"

"I think so, sir," returned Tom, for Jack had told his chum to do the talking, since the discovery was his. "You remember, sir, the old chateau we put out of business the other day?"

"Yes, I recall it. What about it?"

"This: It seems suddenly to have grown a wooded park around it, and the trees and bushes don't seem to be as fresh as natural ones ought to look."

"You mean they camouflaged the ruins, and have put another battery in the old, chateau?"

"I think so, sir. It wouldn't do any harm to drop a few shells there. If it's still a ruin the worst will be that we've wasted a little ammunition and may start the German guns up. And if it is what we think it is, we may blow up the battery."

The commander thought for a moment.

"I'll try it!" he suddenly said. "It's worth all it will cost."

He called an orderly and issued his instructions. Tom and Jack had not yet been dismissed, and now the commanding officer turned to them and said:

"Since you boys were sharp enough to discover this, I'll let you have a front seat at the show which will start soon. Go up and do contact work. Let the gunners know when they make a hit."

The air service boys could not have wished for anything better.

"Once more for our bus!" exclaimed Jack delightedly, when they were outside.

Their Spad had been refilled with gasoline, or "petrol," as it is called on the other side, and oil had been put in, while the machine guns had been looked to.

"You seem to have spotted it all right, Tom," went on Jack, just as they were about to start, for word came that the American batteries were ready.

"Yes, I was looking down through the glass, and when I saw the old chateau it struck me that it had suddenly grown a beard. I remembered it before, as being on a bare hill. I thought it was funny, and that I might be mistaken. But when you agreed with me I knew I was right."

"Oh, the Huns have brought up trees and bushes to disguise the place all right," declared, Jack. "The only question is whether or not the battery is hidden there."

But there was not long a question about that. Their machine was equipped with wireless to signal back the result of the shots, and Jack and Tom were soon in position. From the maps used when they had previously shelled the place to drive out the German gunners, the American artillery forces knew just about where to plant the shells.

There was a burst of fire from the designated battery. Up aloft Jack and Tom watched the shell fall. It was a trifle over, and a correction was signaled back.

A moment later the second shell - a big one sailed over the German first lines, and fell directly on the chateau partly hidden in the woods.

There was a burst of smoke, and with it mingled clouds of dust and flying particles. Faintly to Tom and Jack, above the noise of their motor, came the sound of a terrific explosion.

There had been a direct hit on the old ruins, as was proved by the fact that not only was the German battery put out of commission, but a great quantity of ammunition hidden in the trees and bushes was blown up, and with it a considerable number of Germans.

And that it was a place well garrisoned was evident to the air service boys as they saw a few Huns, who were not killed by the shell and resultant explosion of the ammunition dump, running away from the place of destruction.

"That was it all right," said Jack, as he and Tom landed back of their own lines.

"Yes, and it couldn't have been hit better. I hope that was the battery they wanted put out of business."

And it was, for no more shells came from that vicinity of the

Hun positions for a long time. The aeroplane observations had given the very information needed, and Tom and Jack were congratulated, not only by their comrades, but by the commanding officer himself, which counted for a great deal.

CHAPTER XIII

A DARING SCHEME

Tom sat up on his bunk and looked across at Jack, who was just showing signs of returning consciousness - that is, he was getting awake. It was the morning after the successful discovery of the hidden German battery, and since this exploit the two lads had not been required to go on duty.

"What's the matter?" asked Jack, opening his eyes and looking at his chum. "Has the mail come in? Any letters?"

"No. I was just thinking," remarked Tom, and though his eyes were fixed on Jack it was clear that his thoughts were somewhere else.

"Thinking, Tom? That's bad business. Have you seen the doctor?"

"Oh, shut off your gas!" ordered Tom. "You're side slipping. First you know you'll come down in a tail spin and I'll have to be looking for a new partner."

"It's as serious as all that, is it?" asked Jack, as he began to dress. "Well, in that case I withdraw my observation. Go ahead. How's the visibility?"

"Low. We won't have to go up to-day, unless it clears."

"Um. And I was counting on getting a few Huns right after breakfast. Well, what's your think about, if you really were indulging in that expensive pastime?"

"I was," said Tom, and he got up and also proceeded to put on his clothes. "I was thinking about Harry."

"Oh!" and Jack's voice was decidedly different. It had lost all its flippant tone. "Say, he certainly is in tough luck. I wish we could do something for him - and his sister. Doubtless you were thinking of her, too," and a little smile curled his lips.

"Yes, I was thinking of Nellie," conceded Tom, and he was so bold and frank about it that Jack choked back the joke that he was about to make. "I was thinking that we haven't done very much to redeem our promise."

"But how can we?" asked Jack. "We haven't had a chance to do anything to rescue Harry. Of course I want to do that as much as you do, but how is it to be done? Can you answer me that?"

"We can't do it by just talking," said Tom. "That's what I've been thinking about. A scheme came to me in the night, and I've been waiting to tell you about it."

"Shoot then, my pickled blunderbuss," returned Jack. "I'm with you to the last drop of petrol."

"Well, I don't know that it's so much," said Tom. "It's only that we ought to get word to Harry, somehow, that we're thinking of him and trying to plan some way of rescuing him. We ought to tell him his sister is here, too, and, at the same time we might drop him something to smoke and a cake or two of chocolate."

Jack looked at his chum in amazement. Then he burst out with:

"Say, while you're at it why don't you send him a piano, and an automobile, too, so he can ride home when he wants to? What do you mean - getting word to him? Don't you know that the beastly Huns will hold up the mail as they please, and anything else we might send. They don't even let the Red Cross packages go through until they get good and ready. Talk about your barbarians!"

"Oh, I wasn't thinking of the mail," replied Tom.

"No? What then?"

"Why, we know where he is held a prisoner - at least we have the name of the prison camp, and he may be there unless he's been transferred. Of course that's possible, but it's worth taking a chance on."

"A chance on what?" asked Jack, "You haven't explained yet. What do you plan to do?"

"Fly over the place where Harry is held a prisoner and drop down a package and some letters to him," said Tom. "Now wait until you hear it all before you say it can't be done!" he went on quickly, for Jack seemed about to interrupt.

"If Harry is held where he was first made a prisoner, it's a big place, and there are thousands of our captives there, as well as French and British. Well, where there are so many they have to have a big stockade to pen 'em in, worse luck. And dropping a bomb on a big place is easier than dropping one on a small object."

"Say! Suffering snuffle-boxes!" cried Jack. "You don't mean to drop a bomb in Harry's prison, camp, do you? Do you think he might possibly escape in the confusion?"

"Nothing like that," said Tom. "I mean drop a package containing some smokes, some chocolate and a letter telling him we haven't forgotten him and that we're going to try to rescue him, and for him to be on the lookout. That could be done."

"How?"

"By us flying over the place in our speedy Spad. We needn't make a very big package, though the more of something to eat we can give him the better, for those Boches starve our men. Let's get a week off - the commanding officer will let us go. We can go to our old escadrille and make arrangements to start from there. The boys will help us all they can."

"Oh, there's no doubt about that," assented Jack. "They all liked Harry as much as we did. But I can't see that your scheme will succeed. It's a risky one."

"All the more reason why it ought to succeed," declared Tom. "It's the fellows who take chances who get by. Now let's see if we can get a few hours off to go to Paris."

"Go to Paris? What for?"

"To see Nellie Leroy and have her write her brother a letter. It will be better to have one come direct from her than for us merely to give him news of her in one of our notes."

"Yes," agreed Jack, "I guess it would. And I begin to see which way the wind blows. You wish to see Nellie."

"Oh, you make me tired!" exclaimed Tom. "All you can think of is girls! I tell you I'm doing this for Harry!"

"And I believe you, old top, and what's more, I'm with you from the word go. It's a crazy scheme and a desperate one, but for that very reason it may succeed. The only thing is that we may not get permission to carry it out."

"Oh, I don't intend that anyone shall know what our game is," returned Tom. "Of course the authorities would squash it in a minute. No, we'll have to keep dark about that. All we need is permission to do a little flying 'on our own,' for a while."

"Suppose they won't let us do that?"

"Oh, I think they will, after what we did yesterday," said Tom. "Come on, let's get ready to go to Paris."

CHAPTER XIV

WILL THEY SUCCEED?

The scheme evolved, or, perhaps, dreamed of by Tom Raymond in his anxiety to get some word to the captive Harry Leroy worked well at the start. When he and Jack asked permission to have half a day off to make the trip to Paris it was readily granted. Perhaps it was because of their exploit of the day before, when their sharp eyes had discovered the camouflaged German battery and brought about its destruction, or maybe it was because the day was a misty one,+ when no flying could be done.

At any rate, soon after breakfast saw the two boys on their way to the wonderful city - wonderful in spite of war and the German "super cannon," which had itself been destroyed.

Tom and Jack knew that unless their plans were changed, the two girls and Mrs. Gleason would be at home in Paris, for they had a holiday once in every seven, and it was their custom to come to their lodging for a rest from the merciful, though none the less exceedingly trying, Red Cross work.

Nor had the boys guessed in vain, for when they presented themselves at the Gleason lodging, where Nellie Leroy was also staying, they were greeted with exclamations of delight.

"We were just thinking of you," said Bessie, as she shook hands with Jack.

"And so we were of you," Jack replied, gallantly.

"I thought of it first," said Tom. "He'll have to give me credit for that."

"Yes," agreed Jack, "I will. He's got a great scheme," he added, as Mrs. Gleason came in to greet the boys. "Tell 'em, Tom."

"Is it anything about - oh, have you any news for me about Harry?" asked Nellie eagerly.

"Not exactly news from him, but we're going to send some news to him!" exclaimed Tom. "I want you to write him a letter-a real, nice, sisterly letter."

"What good will that do?" asked Nellie. "I've sent him a lot, but I can't be sure that he gets them. I don't even know that he is alive."

"Oh, I think he is," said Tom, hopefully. "If the German airmen were decent enough to let us know he was a prisoner of theirs, they would tell us if - if - well, if anything had happened to him."

"I think," he went on, "that you, can count on his being alive, though he isn't having the best time in the world - none of the Hun prisoners do. That's why I thought it would cheer him up to let him know we are thinking of him, and if we can send him some smokes, and some chocolate."

"Oh, he is so fond of chocolate!" exclaimed Nellie. "He used to love the fudge I made. I wonder if I could send him any of that?"

Tom shook his head.

"It would be better," he said, "to send only hard chocolate - the kind that can stand hard knocks. Fudge is too soft. It would get all mussed up with what Jack and I have planned to do to it."

"What is that?" asked Bessie Gleason. "You haven't told us yet. How are you going to get anything to Harry through those horrid German lines?"

"We're not going through the German lines we're going above 'em; in an aeroplane. And when we get over the prison camp where Harry is held, we're going to drop down a package to him, with the, letters, the chocolate and other things inside."

"Oh, that's perfectly wonderful!" exclaimed Bessie. "But will the Germans let you do it?"

"Well," remarked Jack, "they'll probably try to stop us, but we don't mind a little thing like that. We're used to it. Of course, as I tell Torn, it's a long chance, but it's worth taking. Of course it isn't easy to drop any object from a moving aeroplane and have it land at a certain spot. We may miss the mark."

"For that reason I'm going to take several packages," put in Tom. "If one doesn't land another may."

"But if you do succeed in dropping a package for Harry in the midst of the German stockade, won't the guards see it and confiscate it?" asked Mrs. Gleason. "You know they'll be as brutal as they dare to the prisoners - though of course,"' she added quickly, as she saw a look of pain on Nellie's face, "Harry may be in a half-way decent camp. But, even then, won't the Germans keep the package themselves?"

"I've thought of that," replied Tom. "We've got to take that chance also. But I figure that, in the confusion, Harry, or some of his fellow prisoners, may pick up the package, or packages, unobserved. Of course there's only a slim chance that Harry himself will pick up the bundle. But it will be addressed to him, and if any of the French, British, or American prisoners get it, they'll see that it goes to Harry all right."

"Oh, of course," murmured Mrs. Gleason. "But what was that you said about the 'confusion?'"

"That's something different," said Tom. "I'm counting on dropping a few bombs on the German works outside the camp, to - er - well, to sort of take their attention off the packages we'll try to drop inside the stockade. Of course while we're doing this we may be and probably shall be, under fire ourselves. But we've got to take that chance. It's a mad scheme, Jack says, and I realize that it is. But we've got to do something."

"Yes," said Nellie in a low voice, "we must do something. This suspense is terrible. Oh, if I only could get word to Harry!"

"You write the letter and I'll take it!" declared Tom.

"And I'll help!" exclaimed Jack.

And then the letters - several of them, for each one wrote a few lines and made triplicates of it, since three packages were to be dropped. The letters, to begin again, were written and the bundles were made up. They contained cigarettes, cakes of hard chocolate, soap and a few other little comforts and luxuries that it was certain Harry would be glad to get.

The rest of the plan would have to be left to Tom and Jack to work out, and, having talked it over with their friends, they found it was time for them to start to their station, since their leave was up at eleven o'clock that night.

Getting permission for a week's absence was not as easy as securing permission to go to Paris. But Tom and Jack waited until after a sharp engagement, during which they distinguished themselves by bravery in. the air, assisting in bringing down some Hun planes, and then their petition was favorably acted on.

Behold them next, as a Frenchman might say, on their way to

their former squadron, where they were welcomed with open arms. They had to take the commanding officer into their confidence, but he offered no objection to their scheme. They must go alone, however, and without his official knowledge or sanction, since it was not strictly a military matter.

And so Tom and Jack were furnished with the best and speediest machine in their former camp, and one bright day, following a hard air battle in which the Huns were worsted, they set out to drop the letters and packages over the prison camp where Harry Leroy was held.

"Well, how do you feel about it?" asked Jack, as he and his chum stepped into their trim machine.

"Not at all afraid, if that's what you mean."

"No. And you know I didn't. I mean do you think we'll pull it off?"

"I have a sneaking suspicion that we shall."

"And so have I. It's a desperate chance, but it may succeed. Only if it does, and we get Harry's hopes raised for a rescue, how are we going to pull that off?"

"That's another story," remarked Tom. "Another story."

They mounted into the clear, bright air, and proceeded toward the German lines. Would they reach their objective, or would they be shot down, to be either killed or made prisoners themselves? Those were questions they could not answer. But they hoped for the best.

CHAPTER XV

BADLY HIT

Before undertaking their kindly though dangerous mission, Tom and Jack had carefully studied it from all angles. At first Jack had been frankly skeptical, and he said as much to his chum.

"You'll never get over the place where Harry is held a prisoner," declared Jack. "And, if you do, and start to dropping packages, they'll never land within a mile of the place you intend, and Harry'll have the joy of seeing some fat German eat his chocolate cake."

"Well, maybe," Tom had agreed, "But I'm going to try."

To this end they had secured the best map possible of the ground in and around the prison camp. Its location they knew from the dropped glove of the aviator, which contained a note telling about Leroy.

It was not uncommon for Germany to disclose to her enemies the names of prisons where certain of the Allies were confined, and this was also done by England and France. The prison camps were located far enough behind the defense lines to make it impossible for them to, be reached in the course of ordinary fighting.

Then, too, the airmen of Germany seemed a step above her

other fighters in that they were more chivalrous. So Tom and Jack felt reasonably certain as to Leroy's whereabouts. Of course it was possible that he had been moved since the note was written, but on this point they would have to take a chance.

To this end they had provided themselves not only with the best maps obtainable showing the character of the ground and the nature of the defenses around the prison, where Harry and other Allied men were held, but inquiries had also been made by those in authority, at the request of Tom and Jack, of German prisoners, and from them had come information of value about the place.

Of course the two air service boys had no hope of inflicting much damage on batteries or works outside the prison. By the dropping of some bombs they carried they hoped to distract attention from themselves long enough to drop the packages to Leroy. The bombs were a sort of feint.

And now they were on their way, winging a path over their own lines, and soon they would be above those of the Hun.

Some of the former comrades of Tom and Jack, having been apprised of what the lads were to attempt, had, without waiting for official orders, decided to do what they could to help. This took the form of a daring challenge to the German airmen to come out and give battle.

After their thorough drubbing of the day before, however, the Boche aviators did not seem much inclined to venture forth for another cloud fight. But the French and some English fliers who were acting with them, laid a sort of trap, which, in a way, aided the two Americans.

A half dozen swift Spads took the air soon after Tom and Jack ascended, but instead of flying over the German lines they went in the opposite direction, making their way to the west. They got out of sight, and then mounted to a great height.

Shortly after this some heavy, double-seated planes set out for the German territory as though to make observations or take photographs. It was the belief of the French airmen that the Huns would swarm out to attack these planes, or else to give battle to the machine in which Tom and Jack rode. And, in such an event, the swift Spads would swoop down out of a great height and engage in the conflict.

And that is exactly what occurred. Torn and Jack had flown only a little way over the trenches of the enemy when they saw some Hun planes coming up to meet them. It was in the minds of both lads that they were in for a fight, but before they had a chance to sight their guns, some French planes of the slow type appeared in their rear.

To these the Huns at once turned their attention, and then the Spads swooped down, and there was a sharp engagement in the air, which ultimately resulted in victory for the Allied forces, though two of the French fliers were wounded.

But the feint had its effect, and attention was drawn away from Tom and Jack, who flew on toward the prison camp.

Had their mission been solely to carry words of cheer with some material comforts to Harry Leroy, it is doubtful if Tom and Jack would have received permission to make the trip. But it was known they were both daring aviators and good observers, and it was this latter ability on their part which counted in their favor. For it was thought they might bring back information concerning matters well back of the German front lines, information which would be of service to the Allies.

And in furtherance of this scheme Jack and Tom made maps of the country over which they were flying. They had been provided with materials for this before leaving.

On and on they flew, changing their height occasionally, and, when they were fired at, which was the case not infrequently, they "zoomed" to escape the flying shrapnel.

But on the whole, they fared very well, and in a comparatively short time they found themselves over the country where, on the maps, was marked the location of Harry Leroy's prison camp.

"There it is!" suddenly exclaimed Tom, but of course Jack could not hear him. However, a punch in Jack's back served the same purpose, and he took his eyes from his instruments long enough to look down. Then a confirmatory glance at the map made him agree with Tom. The air service boys were directly over the prison camp.

This, like so many other dreary places set up by the Germans, consisted of a number of shacks, in barrack fashion, with a central parade, or exercise ground. About it all was a barbed wire stockade and, though the character of these wires did not show, there were also some carrying a deadly electric current.

This was to discourage escapes on the part of prisoners, and it succeeded only too well.

But the camp was in plain sight, and in the central space could be seen a number of ant-like figures which the boys knew were prisoners.

Whether one of them was Leroy or not, they were unable to say.

But they had reached their objective, and now it was time to act. High time, indeed, for below them batteries began sending up shells which burst uncomfortably close to them. They were of all varieties, from plain shrapnel to "flaming onions" and "woolly bears," the latter a most unpleasant object to meet in mid-air.

For the Germans were taking no chances. They knew the vulnerable points of their prison camp lay above, and they had provided a ring of anti-aircraft guns to take care of any Allied, machines that might fly over the place. Whether any such daring scheme had been tried before or not, Tom and Jack could not say.

Of course it was out of the question that any great damage could be done in the vicinity of the camp without endangering the inmates, so it was not thought, in all likelihood, that any very heavy air raids would have to be repelled. But in any case, the Huns were ready for whatever might happen.

"Better drop the bombs, hadn't we?" cried Jack to Tom, as he slowed down the motor a moment to enable his voice to be heard.

"I guess so - yes. Drop 'em and then shoot over the camp again and let the packages fall. It's getting pretty hot here."

And indeed it was. Guns were shooting at the two daring air service boys from all sides of the camp.

In the camp itself great excitement prevailed, for the prisoners knew, now, that it was some of their friends flying above them.

There was another danger, too. Not many miles away from the prison camp was a German aerodrome, and scenes of activity could now be noticed there. The Huns were getting ready to send up a machine - perhaps more than one - to attack Tom and Jack.

It was, then, high time they acted, and as Jack again started the engine, he guided the machine over a spot where the anti-aircraft guns were most active.

"There's a battery there I may put out of business," he argued.

Flying fast, Jack was soon over the spot, or, rather, not so much over it, as in range of it. For when an aeroplane drops a bomb on a given objective, it does not do so when directly above, but just before it reaches it. The momentum of the plane, going at great speed, carries any object dropped from it forward. It is as when a mail pouch is thrown from a swiftly moving express train or a bundle of newspapers is tossed off. In both instances the man in the train tosses the pouch or his bundle before his car gets to the station platform, and the momentum does the rest.

It was that way with the bomb Jack released by a touch of his foot on the lever in the cockpit of the machine. Down it darted, and, wheeling sharply after he had let it go, the lad saw a great puff of smoke hovering directly over the spot where, but a moment before, Hun gums had been belching at him.

"Good! A sure hit!" cried Tom, but he alone heard his own words. Jack's ears were filled with the throb of the motor. He had two more bombs, and these were quickly dropped at different points on German territory outside the camp.

At the time, aside from the evidences they saw, Jack and Tom were not aware of the damage they inflicted, but later they learned it was considerable and effective. However, they guessed that they had created enough of a diversion to try now to deliver the packages containing the letters and other comforts.

Jack swung the machine at a sharp angle over the prison camp, and as he cleared the barbed wire fence Tom, who had been given charge of the packets, let one go. It fell just outside the barrier, caused by some freak of the wind perhaps, and the lad could not keep back a sigh of dismay. One of the three precious packages had fallen short of the mark, and would doubtless be picked up by some German guard.

But Tom had the satisfaction of seeing the two other bundles fall fairly within the prison fence, and there was a rush on the part of the unfortunate men to pick them up.

"I only hope Harry's there," mused Tom. "That's tough luck to wish a man, I know," he reflected, "but I mean I hope he gets the letters and things."

However, he and Jack had done all that lay in their power to make this possible, and it was now time to get back to their own lines if they could. The place was getting too dangerous for them.

Swinging about in a big circle, and noting that groups of prisoners were now gathered about the place where the packets had fallen, Jack sent the machine toward that part of France where they had spent so many strenuous days.

"They're going to make it lively for us!" cried Jack, as he noted two swift German planes mounting into the air. "It's going to be a fight."

But he and Tom were ready for this. Their Lewis and Vickers guns were in position, and they only awaited the approach of the nearest Hun plane to unlimber them. They mounted steadily upward to get beyond the range of the anti-aircraft batteries and were soon in comparative safety, since the Huns, at this particular sector at least, were notoriously bad marksmen.

With the German planes, that would be a different story, and Tom and Jack soon found this out to their cost.

For one of the Boche machines came on speedily, and much more quickly than the boys had believed possible was within range. The German machine guns - for it was a double plane - began spitting fire and bullets at them. They replied, but did not seem to inflict much damage.

Suddenly Tom saw Jack give a jump, as though in an agony of pain, and then the young pilot crumpled up in his seat.

"Badly hit!" exclaimed Tom with a pang at his own heart. "Poor Jack is out of it!"

The machine, out of control for a moment, started to go into a nose dive, but Tom let go the lever of his machine gun, and took charge of the craft, since it was one capable of dual manipulation. Tom now had to become the pilot and gunner, too, and he had yet a long way to go to reach his own lines, while Jack was huddled, before him, either dead or badly wounded.

CHAPTER XVI

JUST IN TIME

It was with mingled feelings of alarm and sorrow that Tom Raymond sent the speedy Spad aeroplane on its homeward way toward the French lines. He was worried, not chiefly about his own safety, but on account of Jack; and his sorrow was in the thought that perhaps he had taken his last flight with his beloved chum and comrade in arms. He could not see where Jack had been hit, but this was because the other lad lay in such a huddled position in the cockpit. Jack had slumped from his seat, the safety straps alone holding him in position, though he would not have fallen out when the machine was upright as it was at present.

"One of those machine gun bullets must have got him," mused Tom, as he started the craft on an upward climb, for it had darted downward when Jack's nerveless hands and feet ceased their control. For part of the steering in an aeroplane is done by the feet of the pilot, leaving his hands free, at times, to fire the machine gun or draw maps.

Tom had a double object in starting to rise. One was to get into a better position to make the homeward flight, and another was to have a better chance not only to ward off the attack of the Hun planes, of which there were now three in the air, but also to return their fire. It is the machine that is higher up that stands the best chance in an aerial duel, for not only can one maneuver to better advantage, but the machine can be aimed more easily with reference to the fixed gun.

In Tom's case he did not have access to this weapon, which was fixed on the rim of the cockpit where Jack could, and where he had been controlling, it. With Jack out of the fight, through one or more German bullets, it was up to Tom to return the fire of the Huns from his swivel mounted Lewis gun. He was going to have difficulty in doing this and also guiding the craft, but he had had harder problems than this to meet since becoming an aviator in the great war, and now he quickly conquered his worrying over Jack, and began to look to himself.

He gave one more fleeting glance at the crumpled-up figure of his chum, seeking for a sign of life, but he saw none. Then he swung about, turning in toward the nearest Hun airman, and not away from him, and opened up with the machine gun, using both hands on that for a moment, while he steered with his knees.

It was not easy work, and Tom hardly expected to make a direct hit, but he must have come uncomfortably close to the Boche, for the latter swerved off, and for an instant his plane seemed beyond control. Whether this was due to a wound received by the aviator, or to a trick on his part was not disclosed to Tom. But the machine darted downward and seemed to be content to veer off for a while.

The third plane Tom soon saw was not going to trouble him, as it had not speed equal to his own, so that he really had left only one antagonist with whom to deal. And this plane, containing two men, with whom he had not yet come to close quarters, was racing toward him at great speed.

"I guess there's only one thing to do," mused Tom, "and that's to run for it. I won't stand any show at all with two of them shooting at me, while I have to manage the machine and the gun too. If I can beat 'em to our lines I'd better do it and run the chance of some of our boys coming out to take care of 'em.

I'd better get Jack to a doctor as soon as I can."

And abandoning the gun to give all his attention to the motor, Tom opened it full and sped on his way. The other machine's occupants saw his plan and tried to stop it with a burst of bullets, but the range was a little too far for effective work.

"Now for a race!" thought Tom, and that is what it turned out to be. Seeing that he was going to try to get away, the Hun plane, which was almost as speedy as the one Tom and Jack had started out in, took after them. The other German craft was left far in the rear, and the one Tom had shot at appeared to be in such difficulties that it was practically out of the fight.

Thus the odds, once so greatly against our heroes, were now greatly reduced, though not yet equal, since Jack was completely out of the game - for how long Tom could only guess, and he seemed to feel cold fingers clutching at his heart when he thought of this.

But Tom soon discovered, by a backward glance over his shoulder now and then, that his machine, barring accidents, would distance the other, and this was what his aim now was. So on and on he sped, watching the German occupied French territory unrolling itself below him, coming nearer and nearer each minute to his own lines and safety.

Behind them, he and Jack - for the latter had done his share before being wounded - had left consternation in the German ranks. The bombs had done considerable damage - as was learned later - and the dropping of packages within the prison camp was fraught with potential danger to an extent at which the Boches could only guess.

On and on sped Tom, sparing time, now and then, to look back at his pursuers, who were, it could not be doubted, doing their best to get within effective range. And, every now and again, Tom would glance at the motionless form of his churn.

But poor Jack never stirred, and Tom was fearing more and more that his chum had made his last flight. As for the Hun aviators, after using up a drum or so of bullets uselessly, they ceased firing and urged their machine on to the uttermost.

But Tom had the start of them, and he was also on a higher level, so that the Germans must climb at an oblique angle to reach him.

And, thanks to this, Tom saw that, if nothing else happened, he would soon be in comparative safety with the unconscious form of Jack. The anti-aircraft batteries were firing in vain, as he was beyond their range, and, far away, he could see the lines of the French armies, behind which he soon hoped to be.

And then the unexpected happened, or, rather, it had taken place some time since, but it was only then brought to Tom's attention. His engine began missing, and when he sought for a cause he speedily found it. Nearly all the gasoline had leaked out of the main tank. As he knew that there had been plenty for the return flight, there was but one explanation of this. A Hun bullet had pierced the petrol reservoir, letting the precious fluid leak away.

"Now if the auxiliary tank has any in it, I'm fairly all right," thought Tom. "If it hasn't, I'm all in."

His worst fears were confirmed, for the auxiliary tank had suffered a like fate with the main one. Both were pierced. There were only a few drops left, besides those even then being vaporized in the carburetor.

With despair in his heart, Tom looked back. If the Hun plane chose to rush him now all would be over with him and Jack. He had only enough fuel for another thousand meters or so, and then he must volplane.

He saw a burst of flame and smoke from the enemy plane, and realized that he was being shot at again. But the distance was still too far for effective aim.

And then, to his joy, Tom saw the pursuer turn and start back toward the German territory. The firing had been a last, desperate attempt to end his career, and it had failed. Either the Huns were almost out of petrol themselves, or they did not relish getting too close to the French lines.

"And now, if I can volplane down the rest of the way, I'll be in a fair position to save myself," mused Tom, as he made a calculation of the distance he had yet to go. It was far, but he was at a good height and believed he could do it.

Suddenly his engine stopped, as though with a sigh of regret that it could no longer serve him, and Tom knew that volplaning alone would save him now. He was still over the enemy country, and had his plight been guessed at by the Germans, undoubtedly they would have sent a machine up to attack him. But they were in ignorance.

There was nothing to do but drift along. Gravity alone urged the craft on. As he swept over the German trenches Tom was greeted with a burst of shrapnel, and he was now low enough to be vulnerable to this. But luck was with him, and though the plane was hit several times he thought he was unharmed. But in this he was wrong. He received a glancing wound in one leg, but in the excitement he did not notice it, and it was not until he had landed that he saw the blood, and knew what had happened.

On and on, and down and down he volplaned until he was so near his own lines, and so low down, that he could hear the burst of cheers from his former comrades.

Then he aimed his craft for a level, grassy place to make a landing, and as he came to a gradual stop, and was surrounded by a score of eager aviators, he cried out, as soon as he could speak, "I'm all right! But look after Jack! He's hurt!"

A surgeon bent hastily over the huddled form, and with the aid of some men lifted it from the cockpit. Jack's legs were covered with blood, and when the medical man saw whence it came, then and there he set hastily to work to stop the bleeding from a large artery.

"You got back only just in time, my friend," he said to Tom, as Jack was carried to a hospital. "Two minutes more and he would have been bled to death."

CHAPTER XVII

A CRASH

Not until a day or so later, when Jack was able to sit up in bed and greet Tom with rather a pale face, did the latter learn all that had happened. And it was a very close call that Jack had had.

As Tom had guessed, it was some of the bullets from the Hun machine gun that had stricken down his chum. One had struck him a glancing blow on the head, rendering Jack unconscious and sending him down, a crumpled-up heap in the cockpit of his machine. Another bullet, coming through the machine later, had found lodgment in Jack's leg, cutting part way through the wall of one of the larger arteries.

It was certain that this bullet, the one in the leg, came after Jack was hit on the head, for that first wound was the only one he remembered receiving.

"It was just as though I saw not only stars' but moons, suns, comets, rainbows and northern lights all at once," he explained to his chum.

The bullet in the leg had cut only part way through the wall of an artery. At first the tissues held the blood back from spurting out in a stream that would soon have carried life with it. But either some unconscious motion on Jack's part, or a jarring of the plane, broke the half-severed wall, and, just before Tom landed, his chum began to bleed dangerously. Then it was the surgeon had made his remark, and acted in time to save Jack's life.

"Well, I guess we made good all right," remarked Jack, as his chum visited him in the hospital.

"I reckon so," was the answer, "though the Huns haven't sent us any love letters to say so. But we surely did drop the packages in the prison camp, though whether Harry got them or not is another story. But we did our part."

"That's right," agreed Jack. "Now the next thing is to get busy and bring Harry out of there if we can."

"The next thing for you to do is to keep quiet until that wound in your leg heals," said the doctor, with a smile. "If you don't, you won't do any more flying, to say nothing of making any rescues. Be content with what you did. The whole camp is talking of your exploit. It was noble!"

"Shucks!" exclaimed Tom, in English, for they had been speaking French for the benefit of the surgeon, who was of that nationality.

"Ah, and what may that mean?" he asked.

"I mean it wasn't anything," translated Tom. "Anybody could have done what we did."

But of this the surgeon had his doubts.

In spite of the dangerous character of his wound, Jack made a quick recovery. He was in excellent condition, and the wound was a clean one, so, as soon as the walls of the artery had healed, he was able to be about, though he was weak from loss of blood. However, that was soon made good, and he and Tom, bidding farewell to their late comrades, returned to the American lines. They had been obliged to get an extension of leave - at least Jack had - though Tom could report back on time, and he spent the interim between that and Jack's return to duty, serving as instructor to the "huns" of his own camp. They were eager to learn, and anxious to do things for themselves.

Before long Jack returned, though he was not assigned to duty, and he and Tom visited Paris and told Nellie, Bessie and Mrs. Gleason the result of their mission.

"You didn't see Harry, of course?" asked Nellie, negatively, though really hoping that the answer would be in the affirmative.

"Oh, no, we couldn't make out any individual prisoner," said Tom. "There was a bunch of 'em - I mean a whole lot - there."

"Poor fellows!" said Mrs. Gleason kindly, "Let us hope that they will soon be released."

"Tom and I have been trying to hit on some plan to rescue Harry," put in Jack. "And we'd help any others to get away that we could. But is isn't going to be easy."

"Oh, I don't see how you can do it!" exclaimed Nellie. "Of course I would give anything in the world to have Harry back with me, but I must not ask you to run into needless danger on his account. That would be too much. Your lives are needed here to beat back the Huns. Harry may live to see the day of victory, and then all will be well."

"I don't believe in waiting, if anything can be done before that." Tom spoke grimly. "But, as Jack says, it isn't going to be easy," he went on. "However, we haven't given up. The only thing is to hit on some plan that's feasible."

They talked of this, but could arrive at nothing. They were not even sure - which made it all the harder to bear - that Harry had received the packages dropped in the prison camp at such risk. The only thing that could be done was to wait and see if he wrote to his sister or his former chums. Letters occasionally did come from German prisoners, but they were rare, and could be depended on neither as to time of delivery nor as to authenticity of contents.

So it was a case of waiting and hoping.

Jack was not yet permitted to fly, so Tom had to go alone. But he served as an instructor, leaving the more dangerous work of patrol, fighting, and reconnaissance to others until he was fit to stand the strain of flying and of fighting once more.

"Sergeant Raymond, you will take up Martin to-day," said the flight lieutenant to Tom one morning. "Let him manage the plane himself unless you see that he is going to get into trouble. And give him a good flight."

"Yes, sir," answered Tom, as he turned away, after saluting.

He found his pupil, a young American from the Middle West, who was not as old as he and Jack, awaiting him impatiently.

"I'm to get my second wing soon, and I want to show that I can manage a plane all by myself, even if you're in it," said the lad, whose name was Dick Martin. "They say I can make a solo flight to-morrow if I do well to-day."

"Well, go to it!" exclaimed Tom with a laugh. "I'm willing."

Soon they were in a double-seater of fairly safe construction – that is, it was not freakish nor speedy, and was what was usually used in this instructive work.

"I'm going to fly over the town," declared Martin, naming the French city nearest the camp. "Well, mind you keep the required distance up," cautioned Tom, for there was, a regulation making it necessary for the aviators to fly at a certain minimum height above a town in flying across it, so that if they developed engine trouble, they could coast safely down and land outside the town itself.

"I'll do that," promised Martin.

But either he forgot this, or he was unable to keep at the required height, for he began scaling down when about over the center of the place. Tom saw what was happening, and reached over to take the controls. But something happened. There was a jam of one of the levers, and to his consternation Tom saw the machine going down and heading straight for a large greenhouse on the outskirts of the town.

"There's going to be one beautiful crash!" Tom thought, as he worked in vain to send the craft up. But it was beyond control.

CHAPTER XVIII

GETTING A ZEPPELIN

Dick Martin became frantic when he saw what was about to happen. He fairly tore at the various levers and controls, and even increased the speed of the motor, but this last only had the effect of sending the machine at a faster rate toward the big expanse of glass, which was the greenhouse roof.

"Shut it off! Shut off the motor!" cried Tom, but his words could not be heard, so he punched Martin in the back, and when that frightened lad looked around his teacher made him understand by signs, what was wanted.

With the motor off there was a chance to speak, and Torn cried:

"Head her up! Try to make her rise and we may clear. I can't do a thing with the levers back here!"

Martin tried, but his efforts had little effect. For one instant the machine rose as though to clear the fragile glass. Then it dived down again, straight for the greenhouse roof.

"Guess it's all up with this machine!" thought Tom quickly. He was not afraid of being killed. The distance to fall was not enough for that, and though he and his fellow aviator might be cut by broken glass, still the body of the aeroplane would protect them pretty well from even this contingency. But there was sure to be considerable damage to the property of a French civilian, and the machine, which was one of the best, was pretty certain to be badly broken.

And then there came a terrific crash. The aeroplane settled down by the stern, and rose by the bow, so to speak. Then the process was reversed, and Tom felt himself being catapulted out of his seat. Only his safety strap held him in place. The same thing happened to Dick Martin.

Then there was an ominous calm, and the aeroplane slowly settled down to an even keel, held up on the glass-stripped frames of the greenhouse, one of the very few in that vicinity, which was considerably in the rear of the battle line.

Slowly Tom unbuckled his safety strap and climbed out, making his way to the ground by means of stepping on an elevated bed of flowers inside the now almost roofless house.

Martin followed him, and as they stood looking at the wreckage they had made, or, rather, that had been made through no direct fault of their own, the proprietor of the place came out, wearing a long dirt-smudged apron.

He raised his hands in horror at the sight that met his gaze, and then broke into such a torrent of French that Tom, with all the experience he had had of excitable Frenchmen, was unable to comprehend half of it.

The gist was, however, to the effect that a most monstrous and unlooked-for calamity had befallen, and the inhabitants of all the earth, outside of Germany and her allies, were called on to witness that never hid there been such a smash of good glass. In which Torn was rather inclined to agree.

"Well, you did something this time all right, Buddie," Tom remarked to Dick Martin.

"Did I - did I do that?" he asked, as though he had been

walking in his sleep, and was just now awake.

"Well, you and the old bus together," said Tom. "And we got off lucky at that. Didn't I tell you to keep high, if you were going to fly over one of the towns?"

"Yes, you did, but I forgot. Anyhow I'd have cleared the place if the controls hadn't gone back on us."

"I suppose so, but that excuse won't go with the C.O. It's a bad smash."

By this time quite a crowd had gathered, and Tom was trying to pacify the excitable greenhouse owner by promising full reparation in the shape of money damages.

How to get the machine down off the roof, where it rested in a mass of broken glass and frames, was a problem. Tom tried to organize a wrecking party, but the French populace which gathered, much as it admired the Americans, was afraid of being cut with the broken glass, or else they imagined that the machine might suddenly soar aloft, taking some of them with it.

In the end Tom had to leave the plane where it was and hire a motor to take him and Martin back to the aerodrome. They were only slightly cut by flying glass, nothing to speak of considering the danger in which they had been.

The result of the disobedience of orders was that the army officials had rather a large bill for damages to settle with the French greenhouse proprietor, and Tom and Dick Martin were deprived of their leave privileges for a week for disobeying the order to keep at a certain height in flying over a town or city.

Had they done that, when the controls jammed, they would have been able to glide down into a vacant field, it was demonstrated. The machine was badly damaged, though it was not beyond repair.

"And that's the last time I'm ever going to be soft with a Hun, you can make up your mind to that," declared Tom to Jack. "If I'd sat on him hard when I saw he was getting too low over the village, it wouldn't have happened. But I didn't want him to think I knew it all, and I thought I'd take a chance and let him pull his own chestnuts out of the fire. But never again!"

"'Tisn't safe," agreed Jack. He was rapidly improving, so much so that he was able to fly the next week, and he and Tom went up together, and did some valuable scouting work for the American army.

At times they found opportunity to take short trips to Paris, where they saw Nellie and Bessie, and were entertained by Mrs. Gleason. Nellie was eager for some word from her brother, but none came. Whether the packages dropped by Tom and Jack reached the prisoner was known only to the Germans, and they did not tell.

But the daring plan undertaken by the two air service boys was soon known a long way up and down the Allied battle line, and more than one aviator tried to duplicate it, so that friends or comrades who were held by the Huns might receive some comforts, and know they were not forgotten. Some of the Allied birdmen paid the penalty of death for their daring, but others reported that they had dropped packages within the prison camps, though whether those for whom they were intended received them or not, was not certain.

"But we aren't going to let it stop there, are we?" asked Tom of Jack one day, when they were discussing the feat which had been so successful.

"Let it stop where? What do you mean?"

"I mean are we going to do something to get Harry away from the Boche nest?"

"I'm with you in anything like that!" exclaimed Jack. "But what can we do? How are we going to rescue him?"

"That's what we've got to think out," declared Tom. "Something has to be done."

But there was no immediate chance to proceed to that desired end because of something vital that happened just about then. This was nothing more nor less than secret news that filtered into the Allied lines, to the effect that a big Zeppelin raid over Paris was planned.

It was not the first of these raids, nor, in all likelihood, would it be the last. But this one was novel in that it was said the great German airships would sail toward the capital over the American lines, or, rather, the lines where the Americans were brigaded with the French and English. Doubtless it was to "teach the Americans a lesson," as the German High Command might have put it.

At any rate all leaves of absence for the airmen were canceled, and they were ordered to hold themselves in readiness to repel the "Zeps," as they were called, preventing them from getting across the lines to Paris.

"And we'll bring down one or two for samples, if we can!" boasted Jack.

"What makes it so sure that they are coming?" asked Tom.

It developed there was nothing sure about it. But the information had come from the Allied air secret service, and doubtless had its inception when some French or British airman saw scenes of activity near one of the Zeppelin headquarters in the German-occupied territory. There were certain fairly positive signs.

And, surely enough, a few nights later, the agreed-upon alarm was sounded.

"The Zeps are coming!"

Tom and Jack, with others who were detailed to repel the raid, rushed from their cats, hastily donned their fur garments, and ran to their aeroplanes, which were a "tuned up" and waiting.

"There they are!" cried Torn, as he got into his single-seated plane, an example followed on his part by Jack. "Look!"

Jack gazed aloft. There was a riot of fire from the anti-aircraft guns of the French and British, but they were firing in vain, for the Zeppelins flew high, knowing the danger from the ground batteries.

Sharp, stabbing shafts of light from the powerful electric lanterns shot aloft, and now and then one of them would rest for an instant on a great silvery cigar-shape - the gas bag of the big German airships that were beating their way toward Paris, there to deal death and destruction.

"Come on!" cried Tom, as his mechanician started the motor. "I'm going to get a Zep!"

"I'm with you!" yelled Jack, and they soared aloft side by side.

CHAPTER XIX

ON PATROL

Aloft with Tom and Jack were several other fighters, for it was not only considered a great honor to bring down a Zeppelin, but it would save many lives if one or more of the big gas machines could be prevented from dropping bombs on Paris or its environs.

The machines which were used were all of the single type, though of different makes and speeds. Each one was equipped with electric launching tubes. These were a somewhat new device for use against captive Hun balloons and Zeppelins and were installed in many of the fighting scout craft of the Americans and Allies.

Between the knees of Toni and Jack, as well as each of the other pilots, was a small metal tube. This went completely through the floor of the cockpit, so that, had it been large enough to give good vision, one could view through it the ground beneath.

In a little rack at the right of each scout were several small bombs of various kinds. Some were intended to set on fire whatever they came in contact with, being of phosphorus. Others were explosive bombs, pure and simple, while some were flares, intended to light up the scene at night and make getting a target easier.

Included in the rack of death and destruction was a simple stick; not unlike a walking cane, and this seemed so comparatively harmless that an uninitiated observer would almost invariably ask its use.

At the lower end of the launching tube, through which the bombs were dropped, was a "trip," or sort of catch, that caught on a trigger fastened to each bomb. The trip pulled the trigger, so to speak, and set in operation the firing device.

In the early days, though doubtless the defect was afterwards corrected, the bombs sometimes stuck in the launching tube, and as they were likely to go off in this position at any moment, it was the custom of the pilots to push them on their way with the cane if the missiles jammed. Hence it was an essential part of each flying machine's armament.

Higher and higher mounted the fighting scouts, with Tom and Jack among their number. It was necessary to mount very high in order to get above the Zeppelins, as in this position alone was it possible for the aeroplanes to fight them to any advantage. The Zeppelins carried many machine guns of long range, and for the pigmy planes to attack them on the same level, meant destruction to the smaller craft.

There were several German machines in the raid toward Paris, but Tom and Jack caught sight of only two. The others were either at too great a height to be observed, or else were farther off, lost in the haze.

But the two silver shapes, resembling nothing so much as huge, expensive cigars, wrapped in tinfoil, were flying on their way, now and then dropping bombs, which exploded with dull, muffled reports - an earnest of what they would do when they got over Paris. They were traveling fast, under the impulse of their own powerful motors and propellers, and also aided by a stiff breeze.

Of course conversation was out of the question among Tom,

Jack and the other aviators, but they knew the general plan of the fight. They were to get above the Zeppelins - as many of them as could - and drop bombs on the gas envelope. They were also to attack with machine guns if possible, aiming at the rudder controls and machinery. It was the great desire of the Allied commanders to have a Zeppelin brought down as nearly intact as possible.

Up and up climbed the speedy scout machines, and it was seen that some of them would never get in a position to do any damage. The German craft were traveling too speedily. But Tom and Jack managed to get to a height of about twenty thousand feet, which was above the Zeppelins, though by this time the Germans were in advance of them, for they had climbed at rather a steep angle. However, they knew their speed was many times that of the German machine on a straight course.

On and on they went. Then came a mist which hid the enemy from sight. The aviators railed at their luck, and Tom and Jack dropped down a bit, hoping to get through the mist. It lay below them like a great, gray blanket.

Suddenly they fairly plumped through it, and saw, not far away, the two big silver shapes, shining in the searchlights which were now giving good illumination. It was a moonlight night, which seemed a favorite for a German bombing expedition.

Far below them, and beneath the Zepplins, Tom and Jack could see the lights of other aeroplanes, which were flying low to observe lanterns on the ground, set in the shape of arrows, to indicate in which direction the German craft were traveling. Later, if necessary, these observing machines could climb aloft and signal to those higher up.

Nearer and nearer Jack and Tom came to one of the Zeppelins. And now, in the semi-darkness, they became aware that they were being fired at by a long-range gun on the

German craft. The bullets sung about them, but though their machines were hit several times, as they learned later, they escaped injury.

Now the battle of the air was on in grim and deadly earnest. Several scout planes flew at the big Zeppelin like hornets attacking a bear. They fired their machine guns, and the Germans replied in kind, but with more terrible effect, for two of the Allied planes were shot down. It was a sad loss, but it was the fortune of war, or, rather, misfortune, for the Zeppelin was not engaged in a fair fight, but seeking to bomb an unfortified city.

Now Tom and Jack, though somewhat separated, were close above the Zeppelin, and in a position where they could not be fired at. They began to drop incendiary bombs through the tubes between their knees.

These bombs were fitted with sharp hooks, so that if they touched the gas bag they would cling fast, and bum until they bad ignited the envelope and the vapor inside. And as they circled about, dropping bomb after bomb, the two air service boys saw this happen. Some at least of their bombs reached their target.

The great craft, now on fire in several places, was twisting and turning like some wounded snake, endeavoring to escape. Tom glanced toward the other Zeppelin and saw that this was fairly well surrounded by aeroplanes, but was not, as yet, on fire.

The bees had fatally stung one great German bear, and, a little later, it crashed to the ground where it was nearly all consumed, and of its crew of thirty men, not one was left alive.

The other plane, though greatly damaged by machine gun fire, was not set ablaze, but was forced to turn and sail for the German lines again. So that two were prevented from bombing Paris.

Well satisfied with what they had accomplished, Torn, Jack and the others who had set the Zeppelin on fire, descended. Later they learned, by word from Paris, that on of the German machines was shot down over that city and some of its crew captured. So that though the Huns did considerable damage with their bombs, they paid dearly for that unlawful expedition.

This was the beginning of a series of fierce aerial battles between the German forces and the Allied airmen, though for a long dine no more Zeppelins were seen. Sometimes fortune favored the side on which Tom and Jack fought, and again they were forced to retire, leaving some of their friends in the hands of the enemy.

Once Tom and Tack, keeping close together doing scout work, were cut off from their companions. They had ventured too far over the Hun lines, and were in danger of being shot down. But a squadron of airmen from Pershing's forces made a sortie and drove the Germans to cover, rescuing the two air service boys from an evil fate.

Then followed some weeks of rainy and misty weather, during which there was very little air work on either side. But the fight on land went on, with attacks and repulses, the Allies continually advancing their lines, though ever so little. Slowly but surely they were forcing the Germans back.

Now and then there were night raids, and once Tom and Jack, who had not flown for a week because of rain, were just back of the lines when a captured German patrol was brought in, covered with mud and blood. There had been lively fighting.

"I wish we were in on that!" exclaimed Tom. "I'm getting tired of sitting around."'

"So am I!" agreed Jack. "Let's ask if we can't go out on patrol some night. It will be better than waiting for it to stop raining."

To their delight their request was granted, as it had been in a number of other cases of airmen. Temporarily they were allowed to go with the infantry until the weather cleared.

The two air service boys were in the dugout one night, having served their turns at listening post work and general scouting, when an officer came in with a slip of paper. He began reading off some names, and when he had finished, having mentioned Tom and Jack, he said:

"Prepare for patrol duty at once."

"Good!" whispered Tom to his chum: "Now there'll be something doing."

He little guessed what it was to be.

CHAPTER XX

CAPTURED

Silently, in the darkness of their trenches, the party of which Tom and Jack were to be members, prepared to go over the top and penetrate the German front line of defense, in the hope of taking prisoners that information might be had of them. It was a risky undertaking, but one frequently accomplished by the Allies, and it often led to big results.

There were about a score in the patrol, and, to their delight, though they rather regretted it later, Tom and Jack were given positions well in front, two files removed, in fact, from the lieutenant commanding.

"Now I suppose you all understand what you're to do," said the lieutenant as he gathered his little party about him in one of the larger dugouts, where a flickering candle gave light. "You'll all provide yourselves with wire cutters, hand grenades and pistols. Rifles will be in the way. Take your gas masks, of course. No telling when Fritz may send over some of those shells. Blacken your faces, as usual. A star shell makes a beautiful light on a white countenance, so don't be afraid of smudging yourselves. And when we start just try to imagine you are Indians, and make no noise. One object is to come in contact with some German post, try to hear what's going on from their talk, and make some captures if we can. Do you all understand German?"

It developed that they did - at least no one would confess he did not for fear of being turned back. But, as it developed, they all had some, if slight, acquaintance with the language.

A little period of anxious waiting followed - a sort of zero hour effect - until finally the word was received from some source, unknown to Tom and Jack, to proceed. The night was black, and there was a mist over everything which did not augur for clear weather on the morrow.

"Forward!" whispered the lieutenant, for they were so near the German lines that incautious talking was prohibited. Out of their trenches they went, Tom and Jack well in front, and close to the leader.

As carefully as might be, though, at that, making noise which the members of the patrol thought surely must be heard clear to Berlin, they made their way over the shell-torn and uncertain ground in the darkness. They went down between their own lines of barbed wire to where an opening had been made opposite what was considered a quiet spot in the Hun defenses, and then they started across "No Man's Land."

It was not without mingled feelings that Tom and Jack advanced, and, doubtless, their feelings were common to all. There was great uncertainty as to the outcome. Death or glory might await them. They might all be killed by a single German shell, or they might run into a German working party, out to repair the wire cut during the day's firing. In the latter case there would be a fight - an even chance, perhaps. They might capture or be captured.

On and on they went, treading close together and in single file, making little noise. Straight across the desolate stretch of land that lay between the two lines of trenches they went, and, when half way, there came from the German side a sudden burst of star shells. These are a sort of war fireworks that make a brilliant illumination, and the enemy was in the habit of sending them up every night at intervals, to reveal to his gunners any party of the enemy approaching.

"Down! Down!" hissed the lieutenant. But he need not have uttered the command. All had been told what to do, and fell on their faces literally - their smoke-blackened faces. In this position they resembled, as nearly as might be, some of the dead bodies scattered about, and that was their intention.

Still each one had a nervous fear. The star shells were very brilliant and made No Man's Land almost as bright as when bathed in sunshine, a condition that had not prevailed of late. There was no guarantee that the Germans would not, in their suspicious hate, turn their rifles or machine guns on what they supposed were dead bodies. In that case-well, Tom, Jack and the others did not like to think about it.

But the brilliance of the star shells died away, and once more there was darkness. The lieutenant cautiously raised his head and in a whisper commanded:

"Forward! Is every one all right?"

"My mouth's full of mud and water - otherwise I'm all right," said some one.

"Silence!" commanded the officer.

Once more he led them forward. They reached the first German wire, and instantly the cutters were at work. Though the men tried to make no noise, it was an impossibility. The wire would send forth metallic janglings and tangs as it was cut. But an opening was made, and the patrol party filed through. And then, almost immediately, something happened.

There was another burst of star shells, but before the Americans had an opportunity to throw themselves on their faces, they saw that they were confronted by a large body of Germans who had come forward as silently as themselves, and, doubtless, on the same sort of errand.

"At 'em, boys! At 'em!" cried the lieutenant. "The Stars and Stripes! At 'em!"

Instantly pandemonium broke loose. In the glaring light of the star shells the two forces rushed forward. There was a burst of pistol fire, and then the fight went on in the darkness.

"Where are you, Tom?"' yelled Jack, as he flung a grenade full at a big, burly German who was rushing at him with uplifted gun.

"Here!" was the answer, and in the darkness Jack felt his chum collide with him so forcefully that both almost went down in a heap. "I jumped to get away from a Hun bayonet," pantingly explained Tom.

Jack's grenade exploded, blowing dirt and small stones in the faces of the chums. There were shouts and cries, in English, French and German. The American lieutenant tried to rally his men around him, but, as was afterward learned, they were attacked by a much larger party of Huns than their patrol.

"We must stick together!" cried Jack to Tom. "If we separate we're lost! Where are the others?"

"Sam Zalbert was with me a second ago," answered Tom, naming a lad with whom he and Jack had become quite friendly. "But I saw him fall. I don't know whether he slipped or was hurt. Look out!" he suddenly shouted.

He saw two Germans rushing at him and Jack, with leveled revolvers. There was no time to get another grenade from their pockets, and Tom did the next best thing. He made a tackle, football fashion, at the legs of the Germans, which he could see very plainly in the light of many star shells that were now being sent up.

Almost at the same instant Jack, seeing his chum's intention, followed his example, and the two Huns went down in a heap, falling over the heads of their antagonists with many a German imprecation. Their weapons flew from their hands.

"Come on! This is getting too hot for us!" cried Jack, as he scrambled to his feet, followed by Tom. "There'll be a barrage here in a minute."

This seemed about to happen, for machine guns were spitting fire and death all along that section of the German front, and the American and French forces were replying. A general engagement might be precipitated at any moment.

The American lieutenant tried to rally his men, but it was a hopeless task. The Germans had overpowered them. Tom and Jack started to run back toward their own lines, having made sure, however, of putting beyond the power to fight any more the two Germans who had attacked them.

"Come on!" cried Tom. "We've got to have reinforcements to tackle this bunch!"

"I guess so!" agreed Jack.

They turned, not to retreat, but to better their positions, when they both ran full into a body of men that seemed to spring up from the very ground in the sudden darkness that followed an unusually bright burst of star shells.

"What is it? Who are they? What's the matter?" cried Tom.

"Give it up!" answered Jack. "Who are you?" he asked.

Instantly a guttural German voice cried:

"Ah! The American swine! We have them!"

In another moment Tom and Jack felt themselves surrounded by an overpowering number.

Hands plucked at them toughly from all sides, and their pistols and few remaining grenades were taken from them.

"Turn back with the prisoners!" cried a voice in German.

The two air service boys found themselves being fairly-lifted from their feet by the rush of their captors. Where they were going they could not see, but they knew what had happened.

They had been captured by the Germans!

CHAPTER XXI

THE CLEW

For one wild instant Tom and Jack, as they admitted to one another afterward, felt an insane desire to attempt to break away from their captors, to rush at them, to attack if need be with their bare hands, and so invite death in its quickest form. They even hoped that they might escape this way rather than live to be taken behind the German lines.

It was not only the disgrace of being captured - which really was no disgrace considering the overwhelming numbers that attacked them - t it was the fear of what they might have to suffer as prisoners.

Tom and Jack, as well as the others, might well regard with horror the fate that lay before them. But to escape by even a desperate struggle was out of the question. They were surrounded by a ring of Germans, several files deep, and each was heavily armed. Then, too, their captors were fairly rushing them along over the uneven ground as though fearful of pursuit. The air service boys had no chance, nor did any of their comrades of the patrol who might be left alive. How many these were, Tom and Jack had no means of knowing. They did not see any of their comrades near them. There were only the Huns who were bubbling over with coarse joy in the delight of having captured two "American pigs," as they brutally boasted.

Stumbling and half falling, Tom and Jack were dragged along. Now and then they could see, by means of the star shells, groups of men, some near and some farther off. There was firing all along the Hun and Allied lines, and as the boys were dragged along the big guns began to thunder. What had started as an ordinary night raid might end in a general engagement before it was finished.

There seemed to be fierce lighting going on between the several detached groups, and the air service boys did not doubt that some word of the dispersing and virtual defeat of the party they were with had reached their lines, resulting in the sending out of relief parties.

"This sure is tough luck!" murmured Jack to Tom, as they stumbled along in the midst of their captors.

"You said it! If our boys would only rush this bunch and get us away."

"Silence, pigs!" cried a German officer, and with his sword he struck at Tom, slightly injuring the lad and causing a hot wave of fierce resentment.

"You wouldn't dare do that if I had my hands free, you dirty dog!" rasped out Tom in fairly good German, and he tugged to free his arms from the hold of a Hun soldier on either side.

The officer who had struck Tom seemed about to reply, for he surged through the ranks of his men over toward the captive, but a command from some one, evidently higher in authority halted him, and he marched on, muttering.

There was sharp fighting between the Hun sentries and small parties, and similar bodies from the American and Allied sides going on along the lines now, and both armies were sending up rockets and other illuminating devices.

The two Virginia lads felt themselves being hurried forward -

or back, whichever way you choose to look at it - and whither they were being taken they did not know. The taunts of their captors had ceased, though the men were talking together in low voices, and suddenly, at something one of them said, Tom nudged Jack, beside whom he was walking.

"Did you hear that?" he asked in so low a voice that it was not heard by the Hun next him. Or if it was heard, no attention was paid to it, for Torn spoke in English. The tramp of the heavy boots of the Huns and the rattle of their arms and accoutrements made noise enough, perhaps, to cover the sound of his voice.

"Did I hear what?" asked Jack.

"What that chap said. It was something about one of the German prison camps having been burned by the prisoners, a lot of whom got away. The rest were transferred to a place not far from here. Listen!"

And the Americans listened to the extent of their ability.

Then it was they blessed their lucky stars that they understood enough of German to know what was being said, for it was then and there that they got a clew to the whereabouts of Harry Leroy, from whom they had heard not a word since the dropping of his glove by the German aviator. They did not even know whether or not their packages had reached their chum.

The talk of the Germans who had captured Tom and Jack was, indeed, concerning the burning of one of the prison camps. As the boys learned later, the prisoners, unable to stand the terrible treatment, had risen and set fire to the place. Many of them perished in the blaze and by the fire of German rifles. The others were transferred to a camp nearer the battle line as a punishment, it being argued, perhaps, that they might be killed by the fire of the guns of their own side.

"And there are some airmen, too, in the new prison camp," said one of the Germans. "Our infantrymen claimed them as their meat, though our airmen brought them down. But there was no room for them in the prison camp with the other captured aviators, so The Butcher has them in his charge."

Tom and Jack learned later that "The Butcher" was the title bestowed, even by his own men, on a certain brutal German colonel who had charge of this prison camp.

Then there came to Tom and Jack in the darkness a curious piece of information, dropped by casual talk of the Huns. One of them said to another:

"One of the transferred airmen tried to bribe me to-day."

"To bribe you? How and for what?"

"He is an accursed American pig, and when he heard we were opposite some of them, he wanted me to throw a note from him over into the American lines. He said I would be well paid, and he offered me a piece of gold he had hidden in the sole of his shoe."

"Did you take it?"

"The gold? Of course I did! But I tore up the note he gave me to toss into the American lines. First I looked at it, though. It was signed with a French name, though the prisoner claimed to be from the United States. It was the name Leroy which means, I have been told, the king. Ha! I have his gold, and the note is scattered over No Man's Land! But I will tell him I sent it into the trenches of his friends. He may have more notes and gold!" and the brute chuckled.

Tom and Jack, looked at one another in the darkness. Could it be possible that it was their friend Harry Leroy who was so near to them, since he had been transferred from a camp far behind the lines?

It seemed so. There were not many American airmen captured, and there could hardly be two of this same rather odd name.

"It must be Harry," murmured Tom.

"I think so," agreed Jack.

"Silence, American pigs!" commanded man officer.

He raised his sword to strike the lad. But just then occurred an interruption so tremendous that all thought of punishing prisoners who dared to speak was forgotten.

A big shell rose screaming and moaning from the Allied lines and landed not far from the party of Germans which was leading along Tom and Jack. It burst with a tremendous noise well inside the Hug defenses, and this was followed by a terrific explosion. As the boys learned later the shell had landed in the midst of a concealed battery - a stroke of luck, and not due to any good aiming on the part of the American gunner - and the supply of ammunition had gone up.

There was great commotion behind the German lines, and two or three of Tom's and Jack's captors were thrown down by the concussion. The air service boys themselves were stunned.

And then there suddenly sounded a ringing American cheer, while a voice, coming from a group of soldiers that confronted the German patrol, cried:

"Halt! Who's there? Are there any of Uncle Sam's boys?"

"Yes! Yes!" eagerly cried Tom and Jack. "Come on! We're captured by the Germans!"

There was another cheer, followed by a roar of rage, and then came a rush of feet. Gleaming bayonets glistened in the light of star shells and many guns, and the members of the German patrol, finding themselves surrounded, threw down their arms and cried:

"Kamerad!"

The fortunes of war had unexpectedly turned, and Tom and Jack had been rescued and saved by a party of Pershing's gallant boys.

CHAPTER XXII

NELLIE'S RESOLVE

"What happened?"

"How'd they get you?"

"Are you hurt?"

These were a few of the questions put to Tom and Jack as they were surrounded by the rescuing party of their friends, led, it afterward developed, by the very lieutenant with whom the two air service boys had started in the patrol across No Man's Land.

The German captors had either all surrendered or been killed, and the tables were most effectively switched around. At first Tom and Jack were too surprised and overwhelmingly grateful to answer.

But they soon understood what had happened. And then they told the story of their fight against odds until captured. They said nothing just then of the unexpected information that had come to them about Harry Leroy's presence in a German camp so comparatively near their own lines. But they resolved, at the first opportunity, to make use of the information.

The shooting of the big guns gradually ceased when it was made manifest that neither side was ready for a general engagement. The pop-pop of the machine weapons, too, died away and the star shells ceased rising.

"Come on you Fritzies - what's left of you," cried the lieutenant, when he had made sure that there were no others of his party whom he could rescue.

Then with Tom and Jack the center of a happy, tumultuous throng of their own comrades, the trip back to the American lines was begun. It was without incident save that on the way a wounded British soldier was found lying in a shell hole and carried in, ultimately to recover.

Tom and Jack told what had happened to them, how they had been surrounded and led away; and then, came the story of the lieutenant who had led the patrol party which had turned defeat into victory with the aid of reinforcements which were sent to him.

He had seen his hopes blasted when rushed by the big crowd of the Hun patrol, and, though slightly wounded, he realized that absolute defeat would come to him and his men unless he could get help. He sent a runner back with word to send relief, and then, surrounding himself with what few men remained alive and uncaptured, the fight went on.

It was bitter and sanguinary, and at last, with only two men left beside him, the lieutenant heard the rush of the relief guard. He was placed in charge, as he knew the lay of the land, and the party hurried to and fro, wiping up little knots of Germans here and there, until the main body encountered the squad having in charge the two air service boys.

"You began to think it was all up with you, didn't you?" asked the lieutenant, when they were all once more safely in the dugout.

"We certainly did!" admitted Tom.

"We had visions of watery soup and wheatless bread for the rest of the war," observed Jack.

He and Tom were slightly wounded - mere scratches they dubbed the hurts - but they were sent to the rear to be looked over and bandaged, as were some of the others who were more severely hurt. There were some who could not be sent back - who were left in No Man's Land silent figures who would never take part in a battle again. They had paid their price toward making the world a better place to live in, and their names were on the Honor Roll.

"Well, what do you think about it?" asked Tom of Jack.

"I don't know what to think. It seems hardly possible that Harry can be so near to us, and yet we can't do a thing to help him."

"I'm not so sure about that," returned Tom. "That's what I want to talk about."

It was a week after the patrol raid, and clear weather had succeeded the rain and mist, so that it was possible for the aeroplanes to operate. And their services were much needed.

There were preparations going on back of the German lines of which General Pershing and the Allied commanders needed to be informed. And only the "eyes" of the armies could see them and report - the eyes being the aeroplanes.

So it came about that, having been relieved of their temporary transfer to the infantry, Tom and Jack were once more with their comrades of the air.

"Well, let's think it over, and talk about it when we come down," suggested Jack. "We've got to go upstairs for our usual tour of duty now."

This would last three hours. They were to do scout work -

report any unusual activity back of the German lines, or give warning of the approach of any hostile aeroplanes. After their tour of duty was ended they would have the rest of the day to themselves, provided there was no general attack. Of course if, while they were up, they were attacked, they must fight.

Each lad had a plane to himself, since the young "huns" had all pretty well passed their novitiate, and were now in the regular flying squad. Later some other new aviators would report for instruction on the battle front.

Up and up climbed Tom and Jack, and eagerly they scanned the German lines for any signs of activity. But though there were some Hun planes in the air, they did not approach to give battle. Possibly some other plans were afoot. Afterward Tom and Jack admitted to one another that there was a great temptation to fly over the German trenches to try to get a sight of the prison that had been spoken of - the camp where Harry Leroy might be held.

But to do this would be in direct violation of their orders, and they dared not take any risks. For to do so might involve not only themselves in danger, but others as well. And that view of the matter determined them. They would have to await their opportunity for rescuing their chum - if it could be accomplished.

Their tour of duty aloft that day was without incident. This is not an usual condition at times along the long battle front. Men can not go on fighting without stop, and there come lulls in even the fiercest battle. Flesh and blood can stand only a certain amount of torture, and then even the soul rebels.

So Tom and Jack drifted peacefully down to their aerodrome, noting that it was being newly camouflaged, for the recent rain had played havoc with some of the concealments.

As far as possible both the Germans and the Allies tried to conceal the location of their flying camps. The aeroplanes and balloons needed large buildings to house them, and such structures made excellent and, of course, fair war-marks for bombing parties in aeroplanes hovering aloft. So it was the custom to put up trees and bushes or to stretch canvas over the aerodromes and paint it to resemble woods and fields in an effort to conceal, or camouflage, the depots where the airships were stationed. But this work was done by a special detail of men, and with it Tom and Jack had nothing to do.

They turned their machines over to the mechanics, who would go carefully over them and have the craft in readiness for the next flight. Then, being free for several hours, the two young airmen could do as they pleased, within certain limits.

"Well, did anything occur to you?" asked Jack, as he and Tom, having divested themselves of their heavy fur-lined garments, went to the mess hall, which was in an old stable, from which the horses had long since been removed.

"You mean a plan to rescue Harry?"

"That's it."

"No, I'm sorry to say I can't think of a thing," Tom answered. "I thought I would, but I didn't. Have you anything to say?"

"Yes. Let's go to Paris."

"You mean to see - er -?"

"Yes!" interrupted Jack with a smile. "This is their day off, and we might as well have a little enjoyment when we can. From the easy time we had to-day we'll have some hard fighting to-morrow. This was too good to last. Heinie is up to some mischief, I think."

"Same here."

So, having received permission, they went to Paris, and soon found their way to the lodgings of Mrs. Gleason, where the air service boys were welcomed by Bessie and Nellie.

Of course the first question had to do with the captive Harry, and to the delight of Nellie Tom was able to say:

"We have news of him, anyhow."

"News? You mean he is all right?"

"Well, as all right as he ever can be while the Boches have him, I suppose," was the answer.

"But the news didn't come direct from him. He's in another camp. I'll tell you about it."

Tom and Jack, by turns, related what had happened on the night patrol, and explained how they had overheard talk of Harry.

"Then he is nearer than he has been?" asked Nellie.

"Yes," admitted Tom.

"Won't it be easier to rescue him then?" Bessie queried.

"Well, that doesn't follow," said Jack. "Of course if we could rescue him, we'd have a shorter distance to bring him, to get him inside our lines. But it's just as difficult getting beyond the German lines now as it was before. Tom and I thought we'd come and talk it over, and see if you girls have anything to suggest. We'll do the rescue work if we only get a chance, and can find some plan. Have you any?"

He asked that question, though he hardly expected an answer. And both he and Tom, as well as Bessie and her mother, were greatly surprised when Nellie exclaimed:

"Yes, I have!"

"You have?" cried Tom. "What is it? Tell us, quick!"

"I am going to save my brother by offering myself as a prisoner in his place," said Nellie with quiet resolve. "That's how I'll save him! I'll exchange myself for him!"

CHAPTER XXIII

THE BIG BATTLE

Nellie Leroy rose from, the chair where she had been sitting, and stood before the little party of her friends, gathered in the little Paris apartment where Bessie Gleason and her mother made their home when they were not actively engaged in Red Cross work. The sister of the captive airman had a quiet but very determined air about her.

"That is what I am going to do," she said, as no one at first answered what had been a dramatic outbreak. "Perhaps you will tell me best how to go about it," and she turned to Tom and Jack. "You know something of the German lines, and where I can best go to give myself up."

"Why - why, you can't go at all!" burst out Tom.

"I can't go?"

"No, of course not. You mean all right, Nellie," went on the young man, "but it simply can't be done. To give yourself up to the Germans would mean for yourself not only - Oh, it couldn't be done!" as he thought of the cruelty of the Huns, not only to the soldiers of the Allied armies but to helpless women and children. "You couldn't give yourself up to those brutes!' he cried.

"To save my brother I could," said Nellie simply. "I would do anything for him!"

"I know you would," murmured Bessie.

"But it would just be throwing yourself away!" exclaimed Jack, coming to the help of his chum, who was gazing helplessly at him in this new crisis. "Tell her, Mrs. Gleason," he went on, "that it is utterly impossible, even if the army authorities would let her. Even if she should give herself up to the Germans, they wouldn't keep any agreement they made to exchange her brother. They'd simply keep both of them."

"Yes, I think they would," said Mrs. Gleason. "It is out of the question, my dear," and gently she laid her hand on the girl's shoulder. "That is very fine and noble of you, but it would be wrong, for it would not save your brother, and you would certainly be made a prisoner yourself. And of the horrors of the German prison - at least some where the infantrymen have been kept, I dare not tell you. I imagine it must be better where the airmen are captured," she went on, for she feared that if she painted too black a picture of what Harry might suffer his sister would not be held back by anything, and might sacrifice herself uselessly.

"But what am I do?" asked Nellie, helplessly. "I want Harry so much! We all want him! Oh, isn't there something? Can't you save him?" and she held out her hands appealingly to Torn and Jack.

There was a moment of silence, and then Tom burst out with:

"Well, I may as well speak now as later, and I'll tell you what I've made up my mind to do. Yes, it's a new plan I've worked out," he went on, as Jack looked at him curiously. "I haven't told even you, old man, as it wasn't quite ready yet. But it's a scheme that may succeed, now that we know definitely where Harry is, from what the German patrol said. He isn't so far away as when we dropped the packages in the prison camp, though we don't yet know that he was there at the time we did our stunt. However, if this new plan succeeds we may have a chance to find out."

"How?" asked Nellie, eagerly.

"By talking to Harry himself."

"How are you going to do that?" demanded Bessie.

"What kind of game have you been cooking up behind my back?" asked Jack.

"As desperate as the other, I guess you'll call it," answered Tom. "But something has to be done."

"Yes, something has to be done," agreed Jack. "Now what is it?"

Tom arose and went to the door. He opened it, looked carefully up and down the hall, evidently to make sure no one was listening, and then came back to join the circle of his friends.

"I'm going to speak of something that very few know, as yet," he said, "and I don't want to take any chances of its getting out. There may be German spies in Paris, though I guess by this time they're few and scattering.

"I'm not going to tell you how I know," he said, "but I do know that soon there is to take place a big battle - that is, it will be big for the American forces that are to have part in it. There has been a conference among the Allied commanders, and it has been decided that it's time to teach the Germans a lesson. They've been despising the American troops, as they despised General French's 'contemptible little army,' and General Pershing is going to show Fritz that we have a soldier or two that can fight."

"You mean there's to be a big offensive?" asked Jack.

"No, I wouldn't go so far as to call it a general engagement like that. It's to be kept within the limits, of the sector where the United States troops are at present," said Tom. "That is where you and I are located, Jack, and that, as you know, is almost opposite the prison where Harry and the others are confined."

"I begin to see what you are driving at!" cried Nellie, her eyes shining. "But are you sure of this?"

"Yes," went on Jack, "how did you bear of this when it's supposed to be such a secret?"

"It came to me by accident," said Torn, "and I wouldn't speak of it to any one but you. Soon, however, it will be more or less public on our side, as it will have to be when we start to get ready. But it's to be kept a secret from Fritz as long as possible. It's to be a surprise attack, and if it doesn't develop into a big battle it won't be the fault of Uncle Sam's boys."

"Will the air service have any part in it?" asked Jack eagerly, as if fearing he might be left out.

"I don't see how they can get along without us," said Tom. "Not that we're the whole works, but it is well established now that an army can't fight without the use of aeroplanes, to tell not only what the other side is doing, but also how our own guns are shooting. Oh, we'll be in it all right!"

"When?" asked Jack.

"That I can't say," replied his chum. "But now to get down to the thing that concerns us, or rather, Harry. I have a scheme - and you can call it wild if you like - that when the battle is going on, you and I, Jack, and some other airmen if we can induce them to do it, and I think we can, may be able to drop bombs near the prison camp. We'll have to judge our distances pretty carefully, or we'll do more harm than good. Then, if all goes well, and we can blow down some of the camp walls or fences, and if the battle favors our side, we can make a descent on enemy territory and rescue Harry and any others that are with him. What do you think of that plan?"

"It's wonderful!" exclaimed Nellie, glaring at Tom with a strange, new light in her eyes.

"It's very daring," said Bessie, more calmly.

"It's crazy!" burst out Jack

"I thought you'd say that," commented Tom calmly, "and I'd have been disappointed if you hadn't. And just because it is crazy it may succeed. But it's the only thing I can think of. Daring will get you further in this war then anything else. You've got to take big chances anyhow, and the bigger the better, I say."

"I'm with you there all right," agreed Jack. "But to land in hostile territory - it hasn't been done ten times since the war began, and have the aviator live to get away with it!"

"I know it," said Tom, quietly. "But this may be the eleventh successful time. Now that's my plan for rescuing Harry Leroy. If any of you have a better one let's hear it."

No one answered, and finally Nellie spoke.

"No," she said, with a shake of her head, "it's very fine and noble of you boys, but I can't allow it. If you wouldn't let me give myself up - exchange myself for Harry, I can't let you give your lives for him this way. It wouldn't be fair. It would be depriving the Allies of two valuable fighters, to possibly get back one, and the possibility is so slim that - well, it's suicidal!" she exclaimed.

"Not so much so as you think," said Tom. "I've got it all figured out as far as possible. And as for landing in hostile territory, if all goes well, and the big battle progresses as

Pershing and his aides think it will, maybe we won't have to land in hostile territory at all. We may drive the Germans back, and then the prison will be within our lines."

"That's so!" cried Jack. "I didn't think of feat. Tom, old man, maybe your scheme isn't as crazy as I thought! Anyhow, I'm in it with you. The only thing is - will this big battle take place?"

"'It will unless the Germans decide to surrender between now and the day set," Tom answered grimly, "and I hardly believe they'll do that. It's a going to be some fight!"

"Glad of it!" cried Jack. "Now we've got something to live for!" As if he and Tom did not risk their lives every day to make life in the civilized world something worth living for.

"Well, we must be getting back!" exclaimed Tom, as he looked at his watch. "All leaves will be stopped in a few days - just before we start preparations for the big battle. If we can we'll see you once more before then."

"And afterward?" inquired Nellie, softly and pleadingly.

"Yes, and afterward, too!" exclaimed Tom. "And we'll bring Harry back with us. Now good-bye!"

It was a more solemn farewell than the friends had taken in some time, for all felt the impending events, and Tom and Jack talked but little during the return trip from Paris to their headquarters.

What Tom had said about the big battle was strictly true. It had been decided in high quarters that it was time the newly arrived American soldiers showed what they could do. That they could fight fiercely and well was not a question, it was only a matter of getting them familiar with the different conditions to be met with on the European battlefields, against a ruthless foe.

Tom and Jack had a chance for one more hasty, flying visit to Paris, and then all leave was withdrawn, and there began in and about the American camp such a period of tense and intensive work as bore out what Tom had said. The big battle was impending.

Great stores were accumulated of rations and munitions. Great guns were brought up into position and skillfully camouflaged. Machine guns in great numbers were prepared and a number of aeroplanes were brought from other sectors and made ready for the flying fight.

"How are your plans coming on?" asked Jack of Tom, at the close of a day when it seemed that every one's nerves were on edge from the strain of preparing.

"All right," was the answer. "I've spoken to a number of the boys, and they're with me. You know we're pretty much 'on our own,' when we're flying, and I think that we can drop the bombs and make a descent long enough to pick up Harry and other refugees if we break open the prison."

"But suppose we land, stall the engines and the Germans surround us?"

"That mustn't happen," said Tom. "We won't stall the engines for one thing. We'll just have to drop down, and taxi around as well as we can until we pick up Harry, or until he sees us. The machines will carry three as well as two, and even if we have, by some mischance to go up in singles, they'll carry double. But I figured on your being with me. Harry knows enough of the game to be on the lookout when he hears the bombs drop and sees the planes hovering over him, and he'll tip off the others to be ready for a rescue.

"Of course I don't say we can get 'em all, and maybe something will happen that we can't get Harry away. But I think we'll teach Fritz a lesson, and I think we can break up the prison camp so some of the poor fellows can get away. As I said, it's a desperate chance, but one we've got to take."

"And I'm with you!" exclaimed Jack. "And now when does the big battle take place?"

He was answered a moment later, for an orderly arrived with instructions to the air service boys to report at their hangars at once.

There they were told something of the impending attack - the first public mention of it, though more than one had guessed something unusual was in the air from the tenseness of the last few days.

The attack was to start at dawn the next morning, preceded by an intense artillery fire. It was to be the fiercest rain of shells since the Americans had come to the front lines. Then the infantry, supported by tanks and aeroplanes, would follow, going over in waves which it was hoped would overwhelm the Germans.

That night was a tense one. Suppose the enemy had guessed, or a spy had given word of the impending battle? Then success would be jeopardized. But the night passed with only the usual exchange of shots and the sending up of star shells over No Man's Land.

And so, as the hour of dawn approached, the tense and nervous feeling grew. Tom and Jack, with their comrades in their hangars, were dressed in their fur garments and ready. Their machines had received the last touches from the hands of the mechanics, and each one was well equipped with bombs and machine gun ammunition. Tom and Jack were to be allowed to go up together in a big double bombing plane.

The night passed. The hour approached. Anxious eyes watched the hands of watches slowly revolve.

Then suddenly, as if the very earth had been blasted away from beneath them, the batteries of big guns belched forth fire, smoke and shell.

The great battle was on!

CHAPTER XXIV

SILENCING THE GERMAN GUNS

Engagements in the World War were on such a vast scale that it was difficult for a single observer to give a word picture of them. All he could see, stationed behind the lines, was a vast cataclysm of smoke and fire, and his ears were deafened by so vast a sound that it was comparable to nothing on this earth ever heard before.

An observer in the air was little better off, save for that portion directly beneath him, and even that he could not see very much of, on account of the smoke and dust. If he looked to the left or the right, or backward or forward, he was at the disadvantage of distance.

To him, then, great columns of infantry appeared only as crawling worms, and batteries of artillery merely patches of woods whence belched fire and smoke. That he must keep high in the air when over the enemy's lines went without saying, for he would be fired at if he came too low. So then, even an airman's vision was limited when it came to describing a great battle.

Of course he always did what he was assigned to do. He kept in contact, or in communication, with his own certain batteries, or his infantry division, directing the shots of the former and the advance of the latter. So, really, he had little time to observe anything save the effect of the firing of his own side on a certain limited objective.

As for the soldiers in battle, they are, of course, unable to observe anything except that which goes on immediately in their neighborhood. The artilleryman fires his gun under the direction of some observer, often far away, who telephones to him to lower or elevate his piece, or deflect it to the tight or left. The infantryman advances as the barrage lifts, and rushes forward according to orders, firing or using his bayonet as the case may be, digging in when halted, and waiting for another rush forward. The machine gunner and his squad aim to put as many of the advancing, retreating, or standing enemy out of the fighting as possible, and to save themselves.

The truck men hasten up with loads of ammunition, fortunate if they are not sent to their death in the drive. The stretcher bearers look for the wounded and hasten back with them.

So, all in all, no single person can observe more than a very small part of the great battle. It is really like looking through a microscope at some organism, while the whole great body lies beyond the field of vision.

Only the general staff-the officers in their headquarters far behind the lines, who receive reports as to how this division or corps is retreating or advancing - can have any real conception of the big battle, and these persons may see it only at a distance.

So the usual process of things in general is reversed, and the person farthest removed from the fighting may really see, or rather know, most about it.

And so with a storm of shot and shell, manmade thunders and lightnings, and bolts of death from the earth below and the air above, the great battle opened and advanced.

It progressed just as other battles had progressed. There was a terrific artillery preparation, which took the Germans evidently by surprise, for the response was long in coming, and then it was not in proportion. After the great cannon had done their best to level the big guns on the German side, a barrage, or curtain of fire was started, and behind this, which was in reality a falling hail of bullets, the Americans and their supporting French and British comrades advanced. The curtain of steel was to kill or push back the Germans, and to make it safe for the Americans to go forward. By elevating the small guns the curtain fell farther and farther into the enemy's territory, thus making it possible for the Allies to go on farther and farther across No Man's Land.

The infantry rushed forward, fighting and dying nobly in a noble cause. Position after position was consolidated as the Germans fell back before the rain of shot and shell. It is always this way in an offensive, small or large. The first rush of the attacking side, be it German, French, British, or American, carries everything before it. It is the counter attack that tells. If the attackers are strong enough to hold what they gain, well and good. If not - the attack is a failure.

But this one - the first great attack of the Americans - was not destined to fail, though once it trembled in the balance.

Tom and Jack, with their companions, had flown aloft, and, taking the stations assigned to them, did their part in the battle. As the light grew with the break of day, they could see the effect of the American big guns. It was devastating. And yet some German batteries lived through it. Several times Tom and Jack, by means of their wireless, sent back corrections so that the American pieces might be aimed more effectively. Below them was a maelstrom - an indescribable chaos of death and destruction. They only had glimpses of it - glimpses of a seemingly inextricable mixture of men and guns.

And through it all, though they did not for a moment neglect their duty, bearing in mind their instructions to keep in contact with the batteries they served, Tom Raymond and Jack Parmly were eagerly seeking for a sight of the prison where

Harry Leroy might be held. At one time after they had dropped bombs on some German positions, thereby demolishing them, Tom, who was acting as pilot, signaled to his chum that he was going far over the enemy's lines to try to locate the prison.

Jack nodded an acquiescence. It was not entirely against orders what they were about to do. They might obtain valuable information, and it would take only a short time, so speedy was their machine. Then too, they had used up all their bombs, and must return for more. Before doing this they wished to make an observation.

Luck was with them. They managed to pass over a comparatively quiet sector of the lines where the German resistance had been wiped out, and where, even as they looked down, Americans were digging in and guns were being brought up to support them.

And not many kilometers inside the German positions from this point, they sailed over a prison camp. They, knew it in an instant, and felt sure it must be the one spoken of by the German who had taken Leroy's gold and then betrayed him.

"That's the place!" cried Tom, though of course Jack could not hear him. "Now to bomb it and set Harry free!"

But they must return for more ammunition, and this they set about doing. They wished they might drop some word to the prisoners confined there, stating that help might soon be on its way to them, but they had no chance to send this cheering word.

Back they rushed to their own lines, and no sooner had they landed than an orderly rushed up to them and instructed them to report immediately to their commanding officer.

"Boys, you're just in time!" he cried, all dignity or formality having been set aside in the excitement of the great battle.

"What is it?" asked Tom.

"We want you to silence some big German guns - a nasty battery of them that's playing havoc with our boys. The artillery hasn't been able to locate 'em - probably they're too well camouflaged. And we can't advance against 'em. Will you go up and try to put them out of business?"

Of course there could be but one answer to this. Tom and Jack hurried off to see to the loading of their machine with bombs - an extra large number of very powerful ones being taken.

Once more they were off on their dangerous mission, for it was dangerous, since many American planes were brought down by German fire that day, and by attacks from other Hun machines.

But Tom and Jack never faltered. Up and up they went, the probable location of the guns having been made known to them on the map they carried. Up and onward they went. For a time they must forego the chance of rescuing their friend.

Straight for the indicated place they went, and just as they reached it there came a burst of fire and smoke. It appeared to roll out from a little ravine well wooded on both sides, and that accounted for the failure of the Americans to locate it. Chance had played into the hands of the air service boys.

There was no need of word between Tom and Jack. The former headed the plane for the place whence the German guns had fired upon the Americans, killing and wounding many.

Over it, for an instant, hovered the aeroplane. Then Jack touched the bomb releasing device. Down dropped the powerful explosive.

There was a great upward blast of air which rocked the machine in which sat the two aviators. There was a burst of smoke and flame beneath them, tongues of fire seeming to reach up as though to pull them down.

Then came a terrific explosion which almost deafened the boys, even though their ears were covered with the fur caps, and though their own engine made a pandemonium of sound.

The air was filled with flying debris - debris of the German guns and men. The bombs dropped by Tom and Jack had accomplished their mission. The harassing battery was destroyed. The German guns were silenced.

CHAPTER XXV

THE RESCUE

Tom and Jack circled around slowly over the place where the German battery had been. It was now no more - it could work no more havoc to the American ranks. It did not need the wireless news to this effect, which the aviators sent back, to apprise the Allies of what had happened. They had seen the harassing guns blown up.

Now out swarmed the Americans, charging with savage yells over the place that had been such a hindrance to their advance. Tom and Jack had done their work well.

There was no need for the one to tell the other what was in his mind. There were still two of the powerful bombs left, and there was but one thought on this matter. They must be used to blow up, if possible, the camp near the German prison. Doing that would create havoc and consternation enough, the air service boys thought, to drive the captors away, and enable Leroy and his fellow prisoners to be saved.

Jack punched Tom in the back and motioned for him to shut off the motor a moment so that talking would be possible. Tom did this, and Jack cried:

"Shall we take a chance?"

"Yes!" Tom answered in return.

Strictly speaking, having accomplished the mission they were sent out on, they should have returned to their base for orders. But the airmen were given more liberty of action and decision than any other branch of the Allied service.

"Go to it!" cried Jack, and once more Tom started the motor and headed the craft for the Hun prison.

Again the air service boys were hovering over the prison camp. They could now see that there was much more activity around it than there had been before the big battery was destroyed. The fight was coming closer, and the Germans evidently knew it. Whether they were trying to arrange to take their captives farther back, or merely seeking to escape themselves from a trap, was not then evident.

And, having reached a position where they could see below them what looked to be a concentration of German guns, perhaps to fire on any force that might advance against the prison. Jack let fall one of his two remaining bombs.

It swerved to one side, and though it exploded with great force, and created havoc and consternation among the Huns, it did not fall where it was intended. The second battery was still intact.

"My last shot!" grimly mused Jack, as he looked at the other bomb.

Tom maneuvered the aeroplane until he had it about where he thought Jack would want it. The latter pressed the releasing lever and the bomb descended. It was the most powerful of the lot, and when it struck and exploded it not only demolished the defensive battery, making a hole in the place where it had stood, but it tore down part of the prison fence, and made such destruction generally that the Germans were stunned.

Instantly, seeing that all had been accomplished that was possible, and noting that hovering around him were other

Allied airmen who had agreed to help in the rescue, Tom sent his craft down. There was a burst of shrapnel around him and Jack, but though the latter was grazed by a bullet, neither was seriously hurt. A Hun plane darted down out of the sky to attack the bold Americans, but quickly it was engaged by a supporting Allied craft. However, the Hun was a good fighter, and won the battle against this antagonist. But when two other Allied planes closed in, that was the last of the enemy. He was sent crashing down to satisfy the vengeance in toll for the life of the birdman ho had taken.

Now Tom and Jack could see that their plan had worked better than they had dared to hope. The boldness of the attack from the air, coupled with the advance of the American army, started a panic in the German ranks. They began a retreat and the regiments near the prison camp were included in the rout.

By this time either some of the prisoners saw that there was a break in the cordon around them, or they realized that a great battle was putting their guards to flight, for some of them made a rush toward a side where there were no Germans, and succeeded in breaking out - no hard task since part of the fence was shattered by the explosion.

"Now's our chance," cried Tom, though of course Jack could not hear this. "Harry may be among that bunch, and we want to get him and any others we can save."

He started the aeroplane on its downward path, while Jack, guessing the object, got the machine gun ready for action, since there might be a squad of Germans ready to give battle on the ground.

Several other planes of the Allies, seeing what was going on, swooped to the aid of the two Americans, for there were no other of the Hun craft within sight now. All had been sent crashing down, or had drawn off.

On either side of the immediate sector which included the

prison camp, the battle was still raging fiercely, mostly with success on the side of the Americans, though in places they suffered a temporary setback.

In the vicinity of the prison itself wild scenes were now being enacted. The prisoners were beginning to rise in force, for they saw freedom looming before them. There were fights between them and the guards, and terrible happenings took place, for the guards were armed and the prisoners were not. But as fast as some of the Germans fell they were stripped of their guns and ammunition, and the weapons turned by the prisoners against their former captors.

All this while Tom and Jack were descending in their plane. As yet they were uncertain whether they were to be able to rescue Leroy or not. They could not distinguish him at that height, though from the enthusiastic manner in which several of the newly liberated ones waved at the on-coming aeroplanes, it would seem that they were of that arm of the service, and appreciated what was about to happen.

Nearer and nearer to the ground flew Tom and Jack. And then, to their horror, they saw that several Germans had set up two machine guns to rake the prison yard, which was still filled with excited captives. The Germans were determined that as few as possible of their late captives should find freedom.

Tom acted on the instant, by sending the plane in a different direction, to enable Jack to use his machine gun. And Jack understood this, for, with a shout of defiance, he turned his weapon on the closely packed Germans around their machine guns.

For a moment they stood and some even tried to swerve the guns about to shatter the dropping aeroplane. But Jack's fire was too fierce. He wiped out the nest, and this danger was averted.

A moment later Tom had the machine to earth, and it ran

along the uneven and shell-torn ground, coming to a rest not far from what had been the outer fence of the prison camp. A group of Allied captives, newly freed, rushed forward. Tom and Jack, removing their goggles, looked eagerly for a sight of Harry Leroy. They did not see him, but they saw that which rejoiced them, and this was more aeroplanes coming to their aid, and also a column of infantry on the march across a distant valley. The stars and stripes were in the van, and at this the rescuers and the prisoners set up a cheer. It meant that the Germans were beaten at that point.

"Where's Harry Leroy? Is he among the prisoners ?" cried Jack to several of the liberated ones who crowded around the machine. There would be no question now of trying to save some one, a rush by mounting to the air with him. The advance of the Americans and the Allies was sufficiently strong to hold the prison position wrested from the Germans.

"Was Harry Leroy among you?" asked Tom, of the joy-crazed prisoners. Many were Americans, but there were French, Italian, Russian, Belgian and British among the motley throng.

Before any one could answer him there was a hoarse shout, and from some place where they had been hiding a squad of German soldiers rushed at the group of recent prisoners about Tom and Jack. Their guns had bayonets fixed, and it was the evident purpose of the Huns to make one last rush on the prisoners near the aeroplane to kill as many as possible.

The Germans were a sufficiently strong force, and none of these prisoners was armed. They began to scatter and run for shelter, and Torn and Jack became aware that matters were not to be as easy as they had expected.

But fortunately the fixed machine gun on the aeroplane, which was near the pilot's seat, pointed straight at the oncoming Huns. With a cry Tom sprang to the cockpit and quickly had the weapon spitting bullets at the foe. Then Jack saw his chance, and, climbing up to his seat, he swung his gun about so that it, too, raked the Germans.

They came on with the desperation and courage of despair, but the steady firing was at last too much for them. They broke and ran - what were left of them alive - in what was a veritable rout, and this ended the last danger for that immediate time and place.

Other aeroplanes dropped down to help consolidate the victory, and the explosion of some American shells at a point beyond the prison camp told its own story. The artillery had moved up to keep pace with the advancing infantry. The big battle had been won by Pershing's men, and the air service boys had not only done their share, but they had been instrumental in delivering a number of prisoners.

As the last of the Germans fled and Tom and Jack leaned back, well nigh exhausted by the strain of the fighting, a voice cried:

"Good work, old scouts! I knew you'd come for me sooner or later. At least I hoped you would!"

They turned to see Harry Leroy walking slowly toward them.

Harry Leroy it was, but wounds, illness, and imprisonment had worked a terrible change in him. He was but the ghost of his former sturdy self. Still it was their chum and the brother of Nellie Leroy, and Tom and Jack knew they had kept the promise made to the sister. They had effected the rescue which the offensive made possible.

"Hurray!" cried Tom. "It's really you then, old scout!"

"What's left of me - yes. Oh, but it's good to see the flag again!" and he pointed to the colors on the aeroplane and on the advancing banners of the infantry. "And it's good to see you again! I'd about given up, and so had most of us, when we heard the shooting and knew something was going on. But how did it happen? How did you get here, and how did you know I was here?"

"Go easy!" advised Tom with a grin. "One question at a time. Can you ride in our bus? If you can we'll take you back with us. The others will be taken care of soon, I fancy, for our boys will soon be in permanent occupation here. Will you come back with us?"

"Will I? Say, I'll come if I have to hitch on behind, like a can to a dog's tail!" cried Leroy, and, weak and ill-nourished as he was, it was evident that the sight of his former comrades had already done him much good.

So now that the position was well won by the Americans and the Allies, Tom and Jack turned their machine about, wheeled it to a good taking off place, and with Harry Leroy as a passenger, though it made the place rather crowded, they flew back over the recent battleground, and to their own aerodrome, where Harry and some other prisoners, brought through the air by other birdmen, were well taken care of.

The great battle was not yet over, for there was fighting up and down the line, and in distant sectors. But it was going well for Pershing's forces.

"And now," remarked Harry, when he had had food and had washed and had begun to smoke, "tell me all about it." He was in the quarters assigned to Tom Raymond and Jack Parmly, being their guest.

"Well, there isn't an awful lot to tell," Tom said, modestly enough. "We heard you were in trouble, and came after you; that's all. How did you like your German boarding house?"

"It was fierce! Terrible! I can't tell you what it means to be free. But I'd like to send word to my folks that I'm all right. I suppose they have heard I was a prisoner."

"Yes," answered Tom. "In fact, you can talk to one of the

family soon. That is, as soon as you can go to Paris."

"Talk to a member of the family? Go to Paris? What do you mean?" Harry fairly shouted the words.

"Your sister Nellie is staying with friends of ours," said Tom. "We'll take you to her."

"Nellie here? Great Scott! She said she was coming to the front, but I didn't believe her! Say, she is some sister!"

"You said it!" exclaimed Tom, with as great fervor as Harry used.

"Didn't you get the bundles we dropped?" asked Jack. "The notes and the packages of chocolate?"

"Not a one," 'replied Harry. "I was looking for some word, but none came, after one of the airmen told me he had dropped my glove. But I knew how it was - you didn't get a chance to send any word."

"Oh, but we did!" cried Tom, and then he told of the dropping of the packages.

But, as Leroy related, he had been transferred from that camp a few days before.

Two of the packets fell among the prisoners, who, after trying in vain to send them to Harry, partook of the good things to eat, which they much needed themselves. They were given to the ill prisoners, and the notes were carefully hidden away. Some time after the war Harry received them, and treasured them greatly as souvenirs.

"But we didn't make any mistake this time," said Tom. "We have you now."

"Yes," agreed Harry with a smile, "you have me now, and

mighty glad I am of it."

A few days later, when Harry was better able to travel, he went to see Nellie in Paris, a message having been sent soon after the big battle, to tell her that he was rescued and as well as could be expected.

"But if it hadn't been for Tom and Jack I don't believe I'd be there now," said Harry to his sister, as he sat in the homelike apartment of the Gleasons.

"I know you wouldn't," said Nellie. "They said they'd rescue you and they did. We shall never be able to thank them enough - but we can try!"

She looked at Tom, and he - well, I shall firmly but kindly have to insist that what followed is neither your affair nor mine.

And now, though you know it as well as I do, my story has come to an end. At least the present chronicle of the doings of the air service boys has nothing further to offer. Their further adventures will be related in another volume to be entitled: "Air Service Boys Flying for Victory."

But it was not the end of the fighting, and Tom and Jack did not cease their efforts. Harry Leroy, too, was eager to get back into the contest again, and he did, as soon as he had sufficiently recovered.

He told some of his experiences while a prisoner among the Germans, and some things he did not tell. They were better left untold.

However, I should like to close my story with a more pleasant scene than that, and so I invite your attention, one beautiful Sunday morning to Paris, when the sun was shining and war seemed very far away, though it was not. Two couples are going down a street which is gay with flower stands. There are two young men and two girls, the young men wear the aviation uniforms of the Americans. They walk along, chatting and laughing, and, as an aeroplane passes high overhead, its motors droning out a song of progress, they all look up.

"That's what we'll be doing to-morrow," observed Tom Raymond.

"Yes," agreed Jack Parmly.

"Oh, hush!" laughed one of the girls. "Can't you stay on earth one day?"

And there on earth, in such pleasant company, we will leave the Air Service Boys.

Choose from Thousands of 1stWorldLibrary Classics By

Ada Leverson
Adolphus William Ward
Aesop
Agatha Christie
Alexander Aaronsohn
Alexander Kielland
Alexandre Dumas
Alfred Gatty
Alfred Ollivant
Alice Duer Miller
Alice Turner Curtis
Alice Dunbar
Ambrose Bierce
Amelia E. Barr
Andrew Lang
Andrew McFarland Davis
Andy Adams
Anna Sewell
Annie Besant
Annie Hamilton Donnell
Annie Payson Call
Annonaymous
Anton Chekhov
Arnold Bennett
Arthur Conan Doyle
Arthur M. Winfield
Arthur Ransome
Atticus
B.H. Baden-Powell
B. M. Bower
Baroness Emmuska Orczy
Baroness Orczy
Basil King
Bayard Taylor
Ben Macomber
Bertha Muzzy Bower
Bjornstjerne Bjornson
Booth Tarkington
Boyd Cable
Bram Stoker
C. Collodi
C. E. Orr
C. M. Ingleby
Carolyn Wells
Catherine Parr Traill
Charles A. Eastman
Charles Dickens
Charles Dudley Warner
Charles Farrar Browne

Charles Ives
Charles Kingsley
Charles Klein
Charles Lathrop Pack
Charles Whibley
Charles Willing Beale
Charlotte M. Braeme
Charlotte M. Yonge
Charlotte Perkins Stetson
Clair W. Hayes
Clarence Day Jr.
Clarence E. Mulford
Clemence Housman
Confucius
Cornelis DeWitt Wilcox
Cyril Burleigh
D. H. Lawrence
Daniel Defoe
David Garnett
Don Carlos Janes
Donald Keyhoe
Dorothy Kilner
Dougan Clark
Douglas Fairbanks
E. Nesbit
E.P.Roe
E. Phillips Oppenheim
Edgar Rice Burroughs
Edith Van Dyne
Edith Wharton
Edward J. O'Biren
Edward S. Ellis
Edwin L. Arnold
Eleanor Atkins
Eliot Gregory
Elizabeth Gaskell
Elizabeth McCracken
Elizabeth Von Arnim
Ellem Key
Emerson Hough
Emily Dickinson
Enid Bagnold
Enilor Macartney Lane
Erasmus W. Jones
Ernie Howard Pie
Ethel Turner
Ethel Watts Mumford
Eugenie Foa
Eugene Wood

Evelyn Everett-green
Everard Cotes
F. H. Cheley
F. J. Cross
Federick Austin Ogg
Ferdinand Ossendowski
Francis Bacon
Francis Darwin
Frances Hodgson Burnett
Frances Parkinson Keyes
Frank Gee Patchin
Frank Harris
Frank Jewett Mather
Frank L. Packard
Frank V. Webster
Frederic Stewart Isham
Frederick Trevor Hill
Frederick Winslow Taylor
Friedrich Kerst
Friedrich Nietzsche
Fyodor Dostoyevsky
G.A. Henty
G.K. Chesterton
Gabrielle E. Jackson
Garrett P. Serviss
Gaston Leroux
George Ade
Geroge Bernard Shaw
George Durston
George Ebers
George Eliot
George MacDonald
George Meredith
George Orwell
George Tucker
George W. Cable
George Wharton James
Gertrude Atherton
Grace E. King
Grace Gallatin
Grant Allen
Guillermo A. Sherwell
Gulielma Zollinger
Gustav Flaubert
H. A. Cody
H. B. Irving
H.C. Bailey
H. G. Wells
H. H. Munro

H. Irving Hancock	James DeMille	Louisa May Alcott
H. Rider Haggard	James Joyce	Lucy Fitch Perkins
H. W. C. Davis	James Lane Allen	Lucy Maud Montgomery
Hamilton Wright Mabie	James Lane Allen	Lydia Miller Middleton
Hans Christian Andersen	James Oliver Curwood	Lyndon Orr
Harold Avery	James Oppenheim	M. Corvus
Harold McGrath	James Otis	M. H. Adams
Harriet Beecher Stowe	James R. Driscoll	Margaret E. Sangster
Harry Houidini	Jane Austen	Margaret Vandercook
Helent Hunt Jackson	Jens Peter Jacobsen	Margret Penrose
Helen Nicolay	Jerome K. Jerome	Maria Edgeworth
Hendrik Conscience	John Burroughs	Maria Thompson Daviess
Hendy David Thoreau	John Cournos	Mariano Azuela
Henri Barbusse	John F. Kennedy	Marion Polk Angellotti
Henrik Ibsen	John Gay	Mark Overton
Henry Adams	John Glasworthy	Mark Twain
Henry Ford	John Habberton	Mary Austin
Henry Frost	John Joy Bell	Mary Catherine Crowley
Henry James	John Kendrick Bangs	Mary Cole
Henry Jones Ford	John Milton	Mary Hastings Bradley
Henry Seton Merriman	John Philip Sousa	Mary Roberts Rinehart
Henry W Longfellow	Jonas Lauritz Idemil Lie	Mary Rowlandson
Herbert A. Giles	Jonathan Swift	M. Wollstonecraft Shelley
Herbert N. Casson	Joseph A. Altsheler	Maud Lindsay
Herman Hesse	Joseph Carey	Max Beerbohm
Homer	Joseph Conrad	Myra Kelly
Honore De Balzac	Joseph E. Badger Jr	Nathaniel Hawthrone
Horace Walpole	Joseph Hergesheimer	Nicolo Machiavelli
Horatio Alger Jr.	Joseph Jacobs	O. F. Walton
Howard Pyle	Julian Hawthrone	Oscar Wilde
Howard R. Garis	Julies Vernes	Owen Johnson
Hugh Lofting	Justin Huntly McCarthy	P.G. Wodehouse
Hugh Walpole	Kakuzo Okakura	Paul and Mabel Thorne
Humphry Ward	Kenneth Grahame	Paul G. Tomlinson
Ian Maclaren	Kenneth McGaffey	Paul Severing
Inez Haynes Gillmore	Kate Langley Bosher	Percy Brebner
Irving Bacheller	Kate Langley Bosher	Peter B. Kyne
Israel Abrahams	Katherine Cecil Thurston	Plato
Ivan Turgenev	Katherine Stokes	R. Derby Holmes
J.G.Austin	L. A. Abbot	R. L. Stevenson
J. Henri Fabre	L. T. Meade	R. S. Ball
J. M. Barrie	L. Frank Baum	Rabindranath Tagore
J. Macdonald Oxley	Latta Griswold	Rahul Alvares
J. S. Fletcher	Laura Lee Hope	Ralph Henry Barbour
J. S. Knowles	Laurence Housman	Ralph Waldo Emmerson
J. Storer Clouston	Leo Tolstoy	Rene Descartes
Jack London	Leonid Andreyev	Rex Beach
Jacob Abbott	Lewis Carroll	Rex E. Beach
James Allen	Lilian Bell	Richard Harding Davis
James Andrews	Lloyd Osbourne	Richard Jefferies
James Baldwin	Louis Tracy	Richard Le Gallienne

Robert Barr	Swami Parmananda	Wilkie Collins
Robert Frost	T. S. Ackland	Willa Cather
Robert Gordon Anderson	T. S. Arthur	Willard F. Baker
Robert L. Drake	The Princess Der Ling	William Dean Howells
Robert Lansing	Thomas A. Janvier	William le Queux
Robert Lynd	Thomas A Kempis	W. Makepeace Thackeray
Robert Michael Ballantyne	Thomas Anderton	William W. Walter
Robert W. Chambers	Thomas Bailey Aldrich	Winston Churchill
Rosa Nouchette Carey	Thomas Bulfinch	Yei Theodora Ozaki
Rudyard Kipling	Thomas De Quincey	Yogi Ramacharaka
Samuel B. Allison	Thomas H. Huxley	Young E. Allison
Samuel Hopkins Adams	Thomas Hardy	Zane Grey
Sarah Bernhardt	Thomas More	
Selma Lagerlof	Thornton W. Burgess	
Sherwood Anderson	U. S. Grant	
Sigmund Freud	Valentine Williams	
Standish O'Grady	Various Authors	
Stanley Weyman	Victor Appleton	
Stella Benson	Virginia Woolf	
Stephen Crane	Walter Camp	
Stewart Edward White	Walter Scott	
Stijn Streuvels	Washington Irving	
Swami Abhedananda	Wilbur Lawton	

www.ingramcontent.com/pod-product-compliance
Lightning Source LLC
Chambersburg PA
CBHW031351170626
46807CB00002B/919